THE OLD MASTERS

Colonel Charles Russell and the man he called Milo had come a long way from their war in the mountains. Russell had been Head of the Security Executive, and now enjoyed retirement and a seat on the board of Commonwealth Mining. But Milo still clung to the reins of dangerous power, in his impossible country the other side of Europe. Now iron ore deposits had been found there, and the question of who would work them could be answered in two very different ways. Milo's answer was to call on Charles Russell; and so after many years Old Masters met, and Charles Russell took a little holiday abroad.

He found the country little changed—prosperous Westernized North, feudal South and semi-barbaric centre, thrown together in uneasy nationhood between East and West. The same violence, the same intrigue, the same air of impending explosion—even some of the original cast. Milo himself, ageing but determined; his wife Gael, who carried her mother's knife with five notches on the handle that would soon be six; his deputy Kamich, dedicated communist and seeker after power. There were new faces too: the American Bentinck and the Armenian Bojalian, watching in their different ways their countries' interests. And among them, again, there was Colonel Charles Russell.

And, in the dusty hills, iron. Or perhaps something more than iron, something which countless times throughout history had provided the decisive spark in the waiting powder, and now would do so again.

THE OLD MASTERS

William Haggard

THE THRILLER BOOK CLUB
LONDON: 1974

The Thriller Book Club
125 Charing Cross Road
London WC2H 0EB

First published 1973

This edition by arrangement with
Cassell & Company Ltd

Printed in Great Britain by
Biddles Ltd, Guildford, Surrey

For
Jessie Suijs

1

Colonel Charles Russell, lately of the Security Executive, wasn't finding his retirement boring. For this there were several sufficient reasons. To begin with he had carefully planned it, not left himself jettisoned, rotting obscurely. He had a pension and a little money, hobbies like golf and some elegant fishing, the good health to enjoy a still vigorous life. Above all he had friends and not all were eminent. Some of them weren't even English. His taste in friends, if not in politics, was liberal and indeed permissive.

He was sitting now waiting for Milo to call. That wasn't his real name or very much like it, for the real one was a jungle of consonants spaced out by uncertain and difficult diphthongs, impossible to the English tongue. He was eminent by any standard but equally he wasn't English. Russell had met him and many others fighting his most irregular war, for when Russell had been a regular officer he'd been considered efficient but also unorthodox. As a result they had sent him on curious missions, dropping him by parachute into countries which were even more so. Greece had been one and Milo's another.

Milo came in and shook hands firmly, a man in his late sixties now but still active and with the air of authority. He said in slightly rusty English:

'It's been far too long since Old Masters met.'

Russell was slightly taken aback. Milo was a Master no doubt, a master of men and a master of politics, but Russell had never thought of himself as any kind of master whatever, simply as an efficient workman. Besides, he didn't much like the wounding adjective. He had a certain age but he seldom felt it and in any case Milo was eight years older.

'Will you take a drink?'

'You know I will.'

A woman was with him and two young men. To the men Milo said in his own harsh language:

'I'm perfectly safe here—an old friend and reliable. But one of you stay outside the door and the other go back to the guards with the car.' They moved and he introduced the woman. 'My wife,' he said. 'I don't think you've met her.'

Russell bowed and as he poured the drinks he inspected her in his Chippendale mirror. He had indeed never met her but knew most things about her. She was a good deal younger than Milo himself, she'd be somewhere in her middle thirties, but she was the daughter of a national heroine, a woman who had fought with her men in the bleak and often profitless hills and had then won another reputation in the even more dangerous world of politics. Though dead now her name was still one of magic and her daughter had not come to Milo dowerless. A marriage of political convenience? Russell, who couldn't be sure, didn't judge. He was content to accept her as female and beautiful.

He turned with the drinks and she took one, smiling. 'Call me Gael,' she said, 'though it isn't my name, any more than Milo's is really Milo.' Her English was rather sharper than his, less formal and more idiomatic. Russell

8

knew she'd once gone to an English school from which she had promptly run away, but even a prison for English young ladies hadn't blunted this blazing beauty's edge. 'I know you find our names impossible and we're perfectly used to approximations. So call me Gael since everyone else does. Not that I'm any sort of Celt.'

'You've a difficult language,' he said.

'All five of them.'

He knew what she meant and smiled politely. Milo's country held five very different races and each of them hated the others bitterly. Two of them weren't much more than minorities but the three great blocks had never fused. Milo had somehow held them together, for though they hated each other's guts they hated the guts of the foreigner harder. Charles Russell knew that Gael was a Southerner whereas Milo was a man of the North. With her mother enshrined in the national pantheon Milo had done shrewdly to marry her.

But then Northerners had always been shrewd. It was one of the reasons the others detested them.

Russell said: 'It was kind to find time to call. You must be rushed off your feet with official engagements.'

The great man accepted another drink. 'You have it a little wrong, I think—this isn't an official visit. No call on Number Ten or the Palace—that is if the Palace would let me in. In point of fact I'm not here at all, just a man who happens to bear my name.'

'But who has to take the same precautions as his namesake still in a distant country.'

'Those guards, you mean? Accept my apologies. They're a nuisance but they're sometimes necessary.'

'So I have heard from time to time.'

'Political assassination is a risk like driving a car in London.'

Russell didn't answer this. There'd been times when this Milo had driven him crazy, his stubbornness and insensate prejudice, but one thing he'd never doubted, his courage. In the mountains he'd managed to keep them fighting, these men of five races and different creeds, often starving, more often without real arms, knowing that if he were captured alive his death would be one which he dare not think of. But he'd held them together and somehow still did, though the timeless feuds ran as deep as ever, now sharpened by international politics. For Milo, like most men of the North, was a realist who looked steadily West. He was hauling a quarter-medieval country into the century it actually lived in, and only the West could help him do that. The men of the Central Province loathed it; they were peasants who looked reluctantly East. Reluctantly because brutal experience had taught them the price of Eastern protection, but in a land where the blood feud was still respectable, indeed in the South it was still a duty, the siren call of racial kinship was more potent than dreary common sense.... Northerners! They were grey materialists. That Milo! He was an alien tyrant. So five times they'd shot and twice they had wounded, but Milo was sitting there, solid, broad shouldered, talking about occupational risks. Whatever he lacked and that was plenty he was patently no form of coward.

Charles Russell broke the silence quietly. 'Then if it isn't an official visit I assume you didn't come just to see me.' This was perfectly true but less than artless. Russell knew very well what Milo had come for.

'I also came to talk to Lord Tokenhouse. As he's chairman of the Board you sit on he'll have told you what it's all about.'

'Not *all* about, though he's dropped a hint. The Board is meeting tomorrow morning and I'm on it as sort of foreign adviser.'

He had taken his time before he'd accepted, for Russell wasn't the sort of *éminence grise* who'd retired to take guinea-pig seats on Boards, nor an out-of-office politician who'd take five thousand a year from anyone provided he gave him sufficient notice to resign before the really big scandal. For one thing those days were almost gone, especially for the civil servants, and as for the retired ambassadors, a protracted but also bitter experience had taught the City they weren't worth tuppence. Somehow they always guessed it wrong, but the need for advice on foreign affairs was a need which big companies had to fill and Charles Russell with his matchless experience could have taken his pick of half a dozen. In the end he had chosen Commonwealth Mining because, as he would blandly explain, its assets were mostly outside the Commonwealth. This he considered wisdom in principle and in the mining world it was simple horse sense. The salary was not enormous but nor were the duties they asked him to shoulder. He advanced no opinions unless invited but he'd already saved his company money by keeping it out of emergent black statelings. Above all things it was another interest in a life which he'd always lived fully and well.

Milo said in his still commanding voice:

'But you mustn't judge this visit wrongly, I have called to try to influence you. If you think our proposition a good one, you'll recommend it to your Board accordingly; if you don't you'll advise them to turn it down.' He gave them his rare but charming smile. 'I know enough about the man Charles Russell to know that a friendship, however longstanding, wouldn't influence him in a matter of duty.'

The words were more than a little formal but the sentiment wasn't insincere. Russell went to the sideboard to pour more drinks and somehow the decanter slipped. It fell not on one of his cherished rugs but straight on the parquet floor where it broke. The glass burst with the sound of a shot from a pistol and in an instant there was a bang on the door.

Russell swore because the fine decanter was remembered from a grandfather's house but he went to the door and opened it quickly. One of the two young men was outside it. He hadn't yet visibly drawn a weapon but Russell would have bet a monkey that he was carrying one underneath his arm. He looked round the room and Milo spoke.

'It's perfectly all right—quite in order. Our host dropped some glass. A domestic accident.'

The young man began a salute but stopped it. Instead he bowed stiffly and left the room.

When Russell came back with another bottle the atmosphere had sensibly changed. The mood of relaxation had gone, in its place was a tension which nagged the nerves. Milo was sitting still as a statue, not frightened for he had never shown fright, but looking, Charles Russell thought, almost sad. And sad, he decided, it truly was. You spent most of your manhood in building a country, and now when you were getting on, a time when you should have been watching the grandchildren, you travelled to London with armed men as your escort. There was more than one word for the man they called Milo. To the idealists in their world of shadows he was simply another fascist dictator, to the hardline communist a contemptible turncoat. Russell considered him neither of these, indeed they were birds of a similar feather. Both had spent lives upon much the same tightrope, on the one side the furnace of total power, on the other the bog of wishful thinking. Man was a very dangerous animal and Russell cared little who ruled him in practice. The enemy was the absence of rule, not the name it had chosen to nail on its bedhead. All one could do was to walk one's tightrope, balancing by the light of *realpolitik*. As Milo had done and look at him now. Yes, man was a very dangerous animal.

Gael was looking at her husband steadily. Russell couldn't read her expression and far less name it. A marriage of convenience, was it? If so she was a very good wife.

He saw that they still wanted time to recover and he walked to the window and parted the curtains. Outside there was a big grey car and Russell's guess was that it was also bulletproof. It carried a British number plate but that meant very little indeed. You could hire such things if you knew where to go, but hardly the men whom Russell saw went with it. Besides the driver there were two more on the pavement, one facing east and the other west. Which was significant in its dismal way. The fourth man was still outside in the lobby.

... Four strongarms and not a sign of the grandchildren.

When he turned from the window he saw they'd recovered. Milo was saying:

'I'm sorry again. It's bad to have to apologize twice.'

'For nothing,' Charles Russell said. 'Forget it.'

'And that man interrupted something important. I told

you I didn't call here to influence you but I don't conceal that I wish I could. This iron is the biggest thing for my country, it could give us a real economic base. Not just tourism—God, I loathe tourism! Hiring your sun and sand to a rabble. It's a form of prostitution really.'

Gael said: 'I hate it too. It's degrading.'

Charles Russell was inclined to agree. 'It's certainly not what your mother fought for.'

'I'm glad you remember my mother.'

'I do.'

'So this ore, you see ...' She left it unfinished.

'If Commonwealth takes it on at all we'll do it on a pretty big scale—enlarge the port, build a feeder railway. I don't think I'm betraying a confidence if I say that we will if we possibly can. Tokenhouse will have told you that. The difficulty is really the money. Have we the finance to do it? It's going to cost a figure which makes me shiver and maybe there'll be a couple of years before a ton goes anywhere near a smelter.'

'You'll realize I couldn't approach the Americans.' Milo's tone conveyed a sharp distaste. 'I'm still enough of an orthodox communist to have prejudices about all things American, and I hope I'm enough of a practical man to have reservations about American business.' It was the old Milo again, decisive and prejudiced. His English was getting less careful with practice, the words were coming back as he used them. 'I don't offer this thing to Commonwealth Mining because a member of its eminent Board once lay out with me and nearly starved. I come to London for a better reason. There's a gambler's chance I shall get a fair deal.'

'You flatter us,' Charles Russell said dryly.

'I don't flatter you and I don't insult you, but you must

handle this or I'll go to the French. And you know how dearly I love the French.'

'This iron ...' Charles Russell began. He stopped. Gael had looked at Milo again and again Russell couldn't read the message. Milo had frowned for a second, then frozen. Something had passed, perhaps a question.

'When are you leaving?'

'Tomorrow evening. Your Board meets at noon so we'll know by then. Lord Tokenhouse has promised to ring me. Like yourself he believes that it's all or nothing.'

'I wish you could stay a little longer. A dinner perhaps, and a quiet theatre.'

'Alas, I'm not really here at all—only a handful know I'm in London. If I were even seen in a public place there'd be every sort of complication.'

'I understand though I'm very sorry.'

Charles Russell rose and went to the door with them. His flat was in fact a maisonette and the door, with three others, led out to a vestibule. The street door was common to all four tenants and went down to the road by a flight of steps. There were the usual Continental politenesses. 'After you.' 'No, after you.' 'I insist.' Gael wouldn't go first and she told them why, laughing. 'My South was once a Turkish *banat* and the women walk second as a matter of course. It's still common in the Middle East.'

'Except, of course, in Libya, where the desert's still full of mines and booby traps.'

It was all very innocent, modestly gay. No one had given a thought to danger.

Charles Russell enjoyed this game within reason but finally he went out first. The others behind saw him check his stride, then suddenly he was back in the room. He shut the door behind him quickly.

'I thought you'd a man outside.'

'I have.'

'You haven't now. He isn't there.'

Gael sat down and produced a radio. Russell had noticed her outsize handbag. She began to talk and a voice answered shortly.

'He hasn't gone back to the car,' she told them.

'And he wouldn't have left his post,' Milo said. He spoke with the quiet but utter conviction of a man who chose his servants carefully.

Charles Russell sat down too. 'I don't like it.'

'It doesn't make sense so we'll have to think.' Milo was in command instinctively. 'What do we know? Who else is living here?'

'Two of the other maisonettes are inhabited by blameless persons. The other is empty, being redecorated.'

'Another entrance, no doubt?'

'There is—through the area. But you said that only a handful of men were in the secret you'd even left your country.'

'I amend that statement since now I must. I *thought* that only a handful knew.'

Charles Russell was silent, thinking professionally. 'If men have got into that empty flat they could have shot us to pieces as we opened the door. We were sitting targets, the guard included. Anyway, why remove the guard? Also I might ask you how.'

'As to the how I do not know. We heard no shot but that means nothing. Nowadays there are other methods, chemical methods, for instance ... so. So he'll be found in some burnt-out crash in the country and I doubt if there'll be a wound on his body.' Milo's shrug was a blend

of regret and acceptance. Life was cheap in his country—
Charles Russell knew it.

But he pursued his line stubbornly. 'Yes, but the *why*?
Why abduct a man when you could shoot all four of us?'

'You forget my friends outside, I think. Start a shoot-up
and even with other exits I doubt if they'd have got away.'

'You haven't quite answered my question, though.'

'You mean why they took him?'

'Yes, I do.'

Milo held up a powerful hand, a single finger raised in
emphasis. 'First to gain time—they're away by now.
There's no point in searching that flat—they'll be gone.'
A second hard finger rose with the first. 'Secondly, and
much more important, they didn't want the guard to *see*.'

'See what?'

'To see what they were doing, of course.' Milo was
being massively patient. He knew more of assassination
than Russell.

'And what were they doing?'

'You've answered that. You didn't mean to but you've
answered it. Libya—mines and booby traps. And perhaps
I could have another whisky.'

Charles Russell brought Milo another whisky and he
raised it in a brief acknowledgement. 'My apologies for
the third time,' he said, 'and this time they are really
serious.' He drank half the whisky, perfectly steady; he
said in his most formal manner:

'I greatly regret to have to inform you that your lobby
is almost certainly booby-trapped.'

Charles Russell sat still and thought it over. Gael sat
in another chair. She was silent. Her hands were clasped
hard in her lap. That was all. Finally Charles Russell
spoke.

'There's the area entrance out through the kitchen.' It sounded easy but he knew it wasn't.

Milo promptly knocked it down. 'Leaving that thing to blow up your neighbours? Or anyone else who may have a key.'

'Then your friends outside?'

'Are simply strongarms.'

'We could ring to the police.'

'And blow the story? That I'm here and am talking to Colonel Charles Russell? Whose reputation in a dangerous world might not fit with a purely social call, to say nothing of finding a bomb in his house. I cannot imagine a greater embarrassment.'

Russell rose in a single, a young man's movement. 'You've convinced me,' he said. 'I'll go and find it.'

'Don't be a perfect bloody fool.' The English was simply colloquial now. 'I know where you come from and whom you fought with when you weren't on odd missions to people like me. You're no sort of bomb disposal man.' He looked at his wife. 'I have your permission?'

'Necessity,' she said. 'And my love.'

It was Russell's turn to be idiomatic. 'You're a very brave fool. I won't let you do it.'

'I've done it before.'

'Thirty years ago.'

'I think I can remember enough.' Milo turned to his wife again, solicitous. 'Please go into the bedroom and stay there—that is if our host will permit the liberty. Get under the bed and lie there quietly. The more amateur these bombers are the more they overload their charges.'

Charles Russell said: 'I'll come with you.'

'That I cannot forbid. It is perfectly proper.' Milo opened the door. 'After you,' he said.

'I accept the honour.'

They took a pace outside and Milo halted, talking to himself reflectively. 'I doubt if it'll be anything fancy— they wouldn't have time for anything fancy. No fuses by noise and far less by our shadows and they wouldn't be able to raise a floorboard without making a commotion and warning us. Just a simple old-fashioned pressure-point, then we walk on it and we all go up.' His eyes were going round the lobby; he stiffened suddenly and turned to Russell. 'Inside that front door is a fibre foot-mat. See anything unusual?'

'No.'

'Not higher than normal?'

'I couldn't say.'

'Is it level with the space which holds it?'

'Yes ... no. Maybe not quite.'

'In this sort of house it ought to lie flat.'

Milo took off his coat and waistcoat, leaving them to lie on the floor. To Russell he said: 'Lie down and keep still. You're here to save your military face. You haven't a hope of being useful.'

He lay down himself and began to edge forward. His backside, Charles Russell found time to reflect, was larger than it had been once, but his courage, if it hadn't increased, had also emphatically not diminished. The head of a sovereign and critical state was crawling about in a Marylebone flat, very possibly blowing them all to eternity. Russell stifled a laugh.

'Keep quiet.'

'I'm sorry.'

'If I've anything against the English it's that their sense of humour is incomprehensible.'

Milo was inching slowly forward and presently Russell

heard him grunt. The tension decreased with the sound, but little. 'It's here,' Milo said. 'I can smell it.'

'Smell it?'

'A figure of speech. Forgive me again.'

Russell lay still and sweated quietly. He'd been taught that all courage was a matter of discipline and discipline was deep in his blood. But Milo had also been brutally frank: Russell was there on his face, breathing dust, since to leave him behind would be simple insult. He wasn't of any use whatever so he wouldn't pretend he could serve where he couldn't. He had never defused a bomb in his life but he had read about the men who did. He considered them very much braver than he was. He raised his head for a second and looked at Milo. He had the mat up now and was staring down at something which seemed to lie below it. Soon he began to talk again but Charles Russell knew that this wasn't garrulity. Milo was talking to ease the strain.

'What was worrying was the anti-handling device, or rather the chance that they'd put one on. But that wasn't very logical thinking. There wasn't any point in doing so—in booby-trapping a simple booby trap. If they didn't get myself and Gael, to destroy someone else would be no compensation.' He stood up carefully and beckoned to Russell. 'Come here, you can see it. But move rather carefully.'

Russell looked down at the doormat's well. There was a metal box about one foot square and maybe an inch and a half in depth.

'With any sort of modern explosive that could blow us to whatever awaits us. Happily it's extremely simple.' Milo pointed but he didn't yet touch. 'Four pressure-points grouped just inside the edges—if you look you can see where the rim compresses. It's not so simple that I can defuse it myself but then I was never sure that I could. But if nobody treads on it nothing will happen.'

He prised up the mine with circumspection and carried it back to Russell's sitting-room. 'It's safe enough but don't stamp your feet.'

'I won't stamp my feet.'

'You were always sensible.'

Milo called out to Gael to join them. To her husband she said: 'I disobeyed you. I sat on the bed but I didn't get under it.' To Russell she said with a housewife smile: 'Don't worry, I put it straight again.'

Russell pointed at the mine. 'What now?'

'I'll talk to the ambassador. The ambassador will know of someone—that's what ambassadors are for.' This time the smile was sardonic, not charming. 'Excellencies are figureheads nowadays, diplomatically almost totally useless. But knowing people is still part of their trade.'

'Someone discreet,' Russell said.

'Of course. I no more want a scandal than you do.' Milo put out his hand. 'We've disturbed you enough.'

Russell led them out to the bulletproof car. Milo said with an utter confidence: 'A man will be calling within an hour. Meanwhile it's been our lucky day.'

'If you call it that.'

'I do. I need luck. And I've had it so far. Evidently I can't have it for ever.'

'You never know.'

'I know,' Milo said.

His wife held her hand out and Russell kissed it. Countries' customs were of great importance, especially a province as old as Gael's. 'You must come out and see us,' she said.

'I'd like to.'

Her husband said with a hint of irony: 'I think I could still guarantee your safety.'

As it happened he was entirely wrong.

In Milo's country Kamich was furious. The President was an ancient puppet, Milo as Premier ruled the country, but there were three Deputy Prime Ministers, each of them chosen from different races, and Kamich came from the Central Province as a balancing weight between North and South. As a Deputy Prime Minister he had been in the secret of Milo's absence, but it wasn't as Milo's deputy that he had planned to have him killed in London.

Nor was it anything personal, a matter of a private rivalry. Kamich didn't think like that—no orthodox communist was even supposed to. In fact he had greatly admired the young Milo and as a boy had borne arms in the war in the mountains. Like all this extraordinary hotchpotch of peoples he sharply mistrusted the other races, but a foreign invasion would have seen him in arms again since mistrust of his fellow citizens was much less than his hatred of all outsiders. Kamich was xenophobic and knew it. It didn't disturb his sleep by a minute. Some twenty million of his countrymen thought exactly the same and considered it natural.

So he'd have fought again but not under Milo, for Milo had chosen the worst of all roads. Accepting the money of shameless tourists—that had been a betrayal but was also forgivable. But bringing the West in to work that iron—that was too much. It was also folly. In a year or two they would be simply a colony, anglicized, tamed, their identity gone. Better cricket, no doubt, than Coca-

Cola, but either would be an importation. Kamich detested importations.

In that lay his problem: he was also a patriot. There was a Power which might back him but not in failure. If he failed it would simply come in and take. Twice before it had almost invaded but hadn't. Kamich didn't want that, he had seen what had happened. He was intelligent and a man of the world, unimpressed by any pan-Slavic theory. If they came then his country as such would be broken. If the West came they'd be a client colony.

It was suddenly and unwelcomely a duty to eliminate Milo. Thereafter the way would not be easy, on the one side an overwhelming Power which mouthed platitudes about agnate blood but behaved when it came like old-fashioned colonialists, on the other the risk of civil war. Milo's power base was in the industrial North, but the South, though much poorer, was also larger. Moreover they were the fighting men, the sinews of a small modern army, as the North provided the State officials. Kamich who came from the Centre loathed both but he didn't desire a civil war. That was his reason for serving with Milo, often resentful but so far loyal. Milo had managed to hold men together.

And now he had betrayed them all, Orthodox, Protestant, Catholic and Muslim. By now these were only labels for interests, but that didn't diminish the gross betrayal. The West was a crumbling façade, degenerate, the East would import a cold alien tyranny. Somehow they'd have to stand alone as somehow they had always contrived to till a softening Milo had sold them all out.

And now he was coming back alive, back to sell out his country for bourgeois profit. Kamich swore softly—not Milo's language. He wasn't a man who was crazy for power, or not for its own sake, far less for its trappings. He wanted power to prevent further prostitution.

Kamich sighed for he couldn't see his way. Events, he suspected, might drive him blindly and as a realist he was frightened of that.

2

Milo had been as good as his word, for in something less than half an hour there was the discreetest of taps on Russell's door. He opened it and a man outside took his hat off as though it had been a drill. 'I think you can guess why I'm here,' he said. 'I don't expect trouble, I've had a description.' The visitor held up a small black bag. 'Simple tools,' he explained. 'It's nothing special.'

He defused the mine coolly, quick and expert. 'It's Czech,' he said, 'as I rather expected. Standard issue and it's now quite safe. You could jump on it if you happened to want to.'

'I don't think I'd fancy that.'

'Quite so.'

'But Czech, I think you said it was? An interesting speculation there.'

'Political speculations, Colonel, are not something which I'm encouraged to make.'

'Then may I offer you a drink?'

'I don't drink as it happens, but not from principle.'

'Then all I can do is thank you.'

'A pleasure.' This time he clicked his heels. 'Good night.'

'Good night and sleep well. You earn your money.'

'If I may say so, sir, you once earned yours harder. If you'd be kind enough to ring for a taxi. I don't want to carry this thing through the streets.'

Charles Russell went to bed and slept, and in the morning his housekeeper brought him tea. His first engagement was not till eleven and he bathed and shaved leisurely, then ate breakfast. There was nothing, he had long since decided, like a solid old-fashioned English breakfast. Dieticians raised horrified hands and deplored it but Charles Russell respected a lifetime's habit.

At a quarter past ten he rang for a taxi and went down to the City to Commonwealth Mining. He was first to arrive and was shown to the boardroom, where he looked round the solid familiar scene, hiding a gently critical smile. For Commonwealth was both old and rich, and they'd done their directors extremely well. Russell knew it was Edwardian baroque, the sibling of a score of such rooms in old-established City Houses, consciously heavy, a trifle pompous, but in its curious way it was also homely. He preferred it by far to Victorian gothic. There was a fine round mahogany table, much older, and in the background a very long sideboard with drinks. Russell helped himself to sherry and sipped it. It was good, as he'd expected it would be, but for Commonwealth that wasn't remarkable.

The directors began to drift in singly, helping themselves to gin and tonics, but Macrae, the accountant, a Scot, took whisky. Charles Russell thought whisky at lunchtime suspect but he was a tolerant man and he liked Macrae who had a dour independence and utter rectitude. When they'd finished their drinks the chairman said: 'Gentlemen.'

They sat down at the table without mischief of precedence—Commonwealth wasn't that sort of firm. Lord Tokenhouse tapped on the table briefly. There was a printed agenda of routine business and they dispatched it in thirteen minutes flat. Only the last item mattered. Tokenhouse spoke again.

'Now the big one.'

None of the six men said a word.

Lord Tokenhouse smiled. 'So I'll have to ask you. It's Mr Shaw to start, I think.'

It was never Christian names in Commonwealth. Commonwealth, though not a colossus, was a hundred years old and properly proud of it.

Shaw was a mining engineer, in his profession a man of unquestioned eminence. 'From my point of view it's a very strong starter. It's been known for some time that the ore was there—the question was whether it was commercially workable. A survey of that sort costs a good deal of money and naturally we've had to be thorough, but even with things which whine and go click it's still a broad guess when it comes to how much. But the content of many samples is high. If it's there in any sort of quantity we should have the Swedes looking sick as dropouts.'

Tokenhouse said: 'I could bear that with fortitude.' He didn't like Swedes nor pretend he did so. He turned to Macrae. 'The finance?' he asked.

Macrae began in his pleasant burr, methodical and always cautious. 'There's more than the actual mining involved, but we all know that and I don't have to press it. There's a port to extend and a railway to build. No passenger service and nothing fancy, but we'll still have to build some sort of railway. In this sort of major operation a road and trucking is not economic.'

'And the money?'

'We could maybe raise two million ourselves.'

'Enough?'

'No, by no means.'

'And the rest?'

'We might find it.'

'I know we could,' Lord Tokenhouse said. 'That's *my* end and of course I've pursued it.'

'Successfully?' somebody asked.

'I think so. What is nowadays called an institution.'

'May I ask which one?'

'You may.' He told them.

There was a silence while they weighed it up. It was a very big name in the City of London. Shaw said at last: 'You're sure?'

'I have told you.' Lord Tokenhouse could be bland as a bishop but at times he could bite like a rattlesnake striking. 'My grandfather founded what's now called Commonwealth. He was a farmer, an Afrikaner Boer, and now I'm a peer of the English realm. But I haven't forgotten my background. No. When I say I have backing you may take it I have.'

'Of course,' Russell said; he was oiling the waters. In a crisis one had to accept confrontations but short of the pinches they got you nowhere. Mistime one and you conceded points.

Relaxed again, Tokenhouse turned to Russell. 'And the political aspect?' he asked. 'You tell us.'

Charles Russell was in no hurry to answer. Lord Tokenhouse was a friend of long standing but there'd been nothing nepotic in joining his Board. Russell was on it for wide experience and there'd been no question of working Milo's iron when Lord Tokenhouse had approached him to join it. But that Russell had lain in the mountains with Milo was now an unexpected bonus and Lord Tokenhouse knew he had bought a bargain. He had all of his race's love of a good one.

'And the political aspect?' he asked again.

'Any communist country is an evident gamble, even in modified form like Milo's. We could sink our assets. They could seize them at any time.'

'So do a lot of non-communist countries—it's one of the risks of contemporary business. There's an excitable little man I won't mention who runs the line he's a hater of communism. And what does he do? He sequesters the lot.'

'That was oil,' Russell said.

'And is iron so different?'

There was something in the bland tone which arrested. The manner was as urbane as ever but Charles Russell's impression was clear and sharp. The chairman knew something the others did not; he was trying to find out if Charles Russell knew too.

'Iron's not so different,' Russell said.

'Then you want to go in?'

'That's not a decision for me to take. But as long as Milo runs the country it strikes me as a very fair gamble.'

'He's sixty-eight.'

'You're sixty-nine.'

'Touché,' Lord Tokenhouse said. 'And after?'

'His wife perhaps—she was once in politics. And she has backing, prestige, in her mother's right.'

'Could she hold it together?'

'If anyone could.'

'I suggest——' Shaw began.

'One moment, please.' Lord Tokenhouse held up a chairman's hand. 'I think Mr Weston has something to tell us.' He looked at the fifth director present. The sixth man was the Secretary, silent. 'Mr Weston, like me, sits on more than one board and his brother's firm are this company's stockbrokers. And Mr Weston has news which he feels he should give us.'

'Not hard news,' Weston said, 'but a strong presumption.' He stared round at the others, enjoying the tension. 'Someone,' he said, 'is having a go at us.'

'Let us have this precise or rule it out.' Lord Tokenhouse swung on the silent Secretary. 'How does the Register stand, or how did it?'

'A month ago it was perfectly normal. Twelve per cent of our shares are in Nominees' names and we don't know the beneficial owner, but they've been held in that way for many years and the Trust is run by a merchant bank. An old-fashioned respectable merchant bank. But in the last four weeks it has notably changed. There's now twenty per cent in a name we don't know about.'

Macrae whistled softly. 'I don't like that.'

'I could ask who in their senses would.' The chairman went back to Weston again. 'The facts first,' he suggested.

'They're not conclusive. What is known is that a firm, not my brother's, has standing orders to buy our equity. The smallest parcel which comes on the market—immediately they snap it up. The price goes up and up of course, and at the moment it's unjustifiably high.'

'Unhealthy,' Lord Tokenhouse said.

'Perhaps sinister.'

'Then those are the facts. And now for the gossip.'

Weston's smile was sardonic. 'Stock Exchange rumours can make you money. They can also lose you the shirt off your back.'

'So we all know, so what's the rumour?'

'The rumour, and I insist it is one, is that the buyer is our friend Mid Western.'

'I'd heard the same story,' Tokenhouse said.

The six men fell into thoughtful silence. Mid Western was an American giant; Mid Western would be a most awkward bedfellow.

'How do you see it?' Lord Tokenhouse asked. 'Seeding the ground for a straightforward takeover? I can tell you I have not been approached.'

'Maybe, but I'm inclined to doubt it. For one thing that isn't Mid Western's form. They're enormous by now but not by takeovers. They've always preferred to buy a stake, then play it hard when the moment suits them.'

'One-fifth is much less than formal control.' It was the Secretary this time, chancing his arm.

Lord Tokenhouse promptly chopped it off. 'I would agree with you that twenty per cent is mathematically less than fifty-one. Nevertheless it's a powerful holding.' He began to reflect aloud for their benefit. 'So a man stands up at a General Meeting and says he's from so-and-so's Nominees. He has twenty per cent of the voting strength and he's casting it in a certain way. Since fifteen per cent of our splendid shareholders neither come to our meetings nor fill in proxies that leaves sixty-five against his twenty. Theoretically that's more than enough, but you still have to swing that sixty-five. With a block of twenty against the board there'd be questions there certainly wouldn't be otherwise. Questions and doubts—a most awkward meeting. At the best any board would be on the defensive. We've never had that before. I detest it.'

'I think the timing's important,' Macrae said quietly.

'Our timing?'

'Mid Western's. They've built up this block in a single month, and anything over a month ago we weren't even thinking of Milo's iron.'

'I follow the thought—it's as shrewd as ever. But what

I don't follow is Mid Western's motive. Mid Western doesn't want iron—it's stuffed with it.' Tokenhouse looked at Russell again, and again Charles Russell's thumbs pricked sharply.

... He does know something the others don't and it's something of real importance too.

'We'll just have to sit it out,' Shaw said. 'There can't be many more shares on the market even if our American friends were planning to go higher than twenty. We'll have to play it by ear till they show their hand.'

'Mid Western, then, you consider irrelevant?'

'It's relevant all right—not decisive.'

'You'd still sign this contract with Milo's government?'

'If you're asking for my vote it is Aye.'

Lord Tokenhouse looked round the fine old table. 'Any dissent?' he inquired.

No one spoke.

'Then we'll enter it as unanimous and feel that we have earned our luncheon.' For the third time he looked hard at Russell; he said on a note of pleasant irony: 'After all, Colonel Russell knows the country. If anything goes wrong we can send him.'

They ate their luncheon with the Managers, smoked salmon, lamb chops and a Camembert cheese, and Charles Russell approved a solid Morgon. Afterwards he went back to his flat, picking up from the now innocuous doormat a letter which had been delivered by hand. It was written on the writing paper of the embassy of Milo's country.

DEAR CHARLES (*if I may still so address you*)

I remember enough of your tastes and habits to know that yet another apology would merely make you very angry, but it's permissible to say I'm pleased that an attaché was at least efficient.

I was a little preoccupied when my wife asked you to visit us. I should have joined myself to the invitation but instead talked nonsense about your safety. In fact I should have pressed our charms. A winter in our stony uplands is very different from our spring by the sea.

The letter was typed and it wasn't signed.

Russell guessed that this somewhat mannered affair was a translation by some embassy hack, but the sentiments he didn't doubt. Milo was now a Head of State, or since the existence of a shadowy President made that statement incorrect in principle, Milo was the man who ran it. But their friendship had not been soured by that. In more than one way Charles Russell was tempted. But one should never go back, it was never the same.

He replied with polite but quite firm regrets. His doctor, he said, would alas not permit it.

He called in a doctor just once a year when he wanted his annual medical check.

3

Kamich was under increasing pressure, in a position which, when he looked at it coolly, he suspected was a contradiction. Somehow his country must stand alone as somehow it had always contrived to till Milo had taken the easy road. That was simple to think but not to do. To treble his country's foreign earnings by selling iron ore to much richer states was something which Kamich was prepared to forgo since he believed that the political price would in fact be his country's total dependence. The real point was whether he *could* forgo it. This wasn't a choice between cricket and Cola, it was one between cricket and Cola on one side and a Power which he feared more than death on the other.

His relationship with that Power was a split one, the contradiction in his political loyalties a reflection of his private thinking. He was still a hardline communist, or as hard as any man could be who was also at heart an old-fashioned patriot, and for selling his country's iron to the West Milo was deeply and bitterly suspect. It had been made extremely clear to Kamich that if he managed to topple Milo by coup he'd be supported in very practical ways, but it was precisely those practical ways which he feared. In his boyhood he had seen bitter fighting, and if he did what his own Central Province urged him, tried to throw down Milo by coup or cunning, then the result could be a civil war which could lose them a generation of men and twenty-nine years of material progress. In the end that could only finish one way: that other Power would destroy them all equally.

So his problem was displacing Milo, his problem and as he saw it his duty, but to do that by force was out of the question when the South and the army were fiercely against him. Just killing him would be fairly easy, he'd been close to death several times before, but the moment would have to be picked with discretion if the repercussions were not to be worse politically than allowing him to sell them out. Milo's visit to London had been the chance of a lifetime since the impact would have been lessened by distance and suspicion would be diffused and uncertain. Some curious persons walked freely in London and the British police were clearly incompetent, hamstrung by the preposterous theory that you couldn't put a man away without the evidence a court would act on. Kamich had even roughed out a story, for there were plenty of refugees in England. He'd have released it to the Press of the world; he'd have protested to the British government in terms of the utmost indignation; in the end he'd have broken off relations, thereby, he thought grimly, killing more than one bird. For Commonwealth would renege on its bargain. No sensible man sank large sums of capital in a country which had expelled his ambassador.

All this he would have done as Premier for he was the senior of three established Deputies, and provided succession wasn't challenged, by chaos or by civil war, he was something approaching the natural heir. But now he wasn't Premier—no; he was a man in a rapidly worsening crisis.

For the news from London was very bad. Not only had

Milo escaped alive from the trap which might have disposed of him without raising a local political storm but he'd decided to sign that treacherous contract. For a moment Kamich allowed himself hope since that wasn't in itself a fatality. Let them come in and enlarge the port —one could always make use of a bigger port. Let them come in and build their railway. Let them even lay down their installations. In a year or two he'd arrange some quarrel, some dispute about the royalties due, then he'd squeeze them out and finally nationalize. The precedents were clearly established. If Commonwealth chose to take foolish risks Kamich wasn't the man to protect capitalists.

So he'd be left with the iron and the means to work it. A perfect solution. Alas, not quite. They might stop him from selling the iron in the market, and recent events in the world of oil suggested they might succeed in just that, but worse, they might not consent to be robbed. Kamich was an orthodox communist who'd absorbed the pure milk of doctrine gladly. Great international corporations were capitalism in its most dangerous form. They paid a lip service to free competition but secretly they were quietly incestuous with cross-holdings in each others' equities and directors on each others' boards. Kamich didn't fear a British company—no contemporary British government would risk action for a commercial asset—but he didn't believe, as a matter of principle, that Commonwealth would be purely British. There were other peoples, not yet degenerate, unsubtle perhaps—not the worse for that. If they landed Marines to protect their bananas God knew what they'd do when it came to iron.

Kamich nodded. That was orthodox thinking.

There was also a man called Richard Bentinck, a respected and even popular consul. He was a respected and even popular consul but he was also something very different. Kamich did not resent the fact, it was the common and contemporary practice, and he hadn't a stiffnecked Liberal Press to protest against what it considered irregular. His friends to the east had started it, these men with diplomatic cover, and now there was hardly a country in Europe without a man on the List in some foreign capital who hadn't also a very different profession. The Americans hadn't invented the system, they invented things surprisingly seldom, but they'd caught on fast and were great improvers. Richard Bentinck had behind his shoulder an almost autonomous Power which was not one. Not with a capital P, that is, but capitals wouldn't increase its influence nor diminish it by their formal absence.

And so far Bentinck had shown no interest, though that didn't mean that he'd never cut in. If one of his country's corporations had an active interest in Commonwealth Mining and if one of his country's corporations was in danger of losing a foreign-based asset, then he'd certainly take a hand and play it. Not Marines perhaps—that was rather old hat and too adjacent to another great Power. But there were very uncomfortable things he could do. There was publicly accounted aid, the country might do without that if it had to, but there was also the secret subsidy which they drew whilst they held their eastern frontier. If that went they'd be in serious trouble. Like all politics this was a balancing act.

He dismissed Richard Bentinck from thought uneasily for he feared being made to meet other men's moves and Bentinck had so far held his hand up. In any case Kamich had no information, no certainty that Bentinck's country had any real stake in Commonwealth Mining. Till that emerged, if it ever did, it was Commonwealth he must overtly deal with.

And Commonwealth might be sufficiently formidable, they had most of it running strongly for them. They had a director called Russell, an old friend of Milo's, and Milo was still very much in the saddle. It was likely that the next move they made would be to send out someone who really mattered, not another technician, they'd had all those, but someone whose voice would surely be heeded. Charles Russell was the obvious man by both ancient connection and wide repute. If anyone knew this country he did.

Kamich lit one of his short cheroots. He had met Colonel Russell in days which were gone, though he doubted that he'd recall the occasion. Very English the boy who'd been Kamich had thought him, but it was stupid not to acknowledge their virtues. They weren't an alarmingly clever people but they owned a sort of instinctive horse sense which served them much better than mere intelligence. It was intelligence which in fact was destroying them, their intellectuals' passion for chatter. Above all things they were mostly reasonable and Kamich proposed to play on that. He had decided by now that he couldn't stop Commonwealth: instead he would bait the hook with reason, let them in on fair terms and then grab the lot. But Charles Russell was the danger here, he had experience, local knowledge and instinct. There were methods of dealing with men like that but in Russell's case they were not available. Kamich would doublecross Commonwealth happily but he had private and imperative reasons why he couldn't do violence to Colonel Charles Russell.

If he came he might not be staying with Milo but in a hotel by the mild and shining sea, three hours by road to the dusty capital. As Foreign Minister among other things it would be perfectly proper for Kamich to call on him, welcoming the distinguished guest and conveying perhaps the discreetest of warnings. You are welcome here as Milo's guest but a guest has his obligations. Watch them.

Kamich frowned for he wasn't entirely happy. It looked manageable but it might not turn out so. For the second time a foreboding gripped him that events would be shaping his course, not Kamich.

Charles Russell was in a rare bad temper since he'd lunched at his club and been caught by a bore. Not the common or garden and known club bore for whom the members had an established technique, but the diplomatic bore *pur sang*. Russell had friends who were civil servants but diplomats he mostly disliked. He would have admitted that this might well be prejudice, but it was prejudice backed by observation. Their airs and affectations annoyed him and their manner of a race apart. Moreover they weren't very good at their job, which at bottom was gaining information. Charles Russell had been a distinguished interrogator, and in this delicate and difficult business where a single word wrong or the wrong sort of look could shut a man's mouth and keep it buttoned, he considered the average diplomat clumsy.

This one had been a man in the Foreign Office and what he'd wanted to know was the real hard news. Charles Russell had been in no way surprised—Sir Jonathan's sources were known to be suspect since in fact they were only men like himself—but he'd wanted his information free; he hadn't even offered a drink but had borne down with an air of the old boy network and a sort of self-conscious grisly bonhomie which was as specious as his brushed-up moustache.

Some preliminaries about nothing at all, how the club had changed and much for the worse, then the question delivered directly, naked.

What did Charles Russell really think was the present position in Milo's country?

He had answered he hadn't the least idea.

But he'd been there, he knew it very well.

'I was there in the war,' Charles Russell said. 'That was twenty-five years ago and more. Twenty-nine if you wish to be wholly accurate.'

But he'd kept in touch with a friend he'd made, a man who was now of great importance.

'If you mean Milo, I've kept in touch. Meanwhile he has held the country together.'

'A remarkable man.'

... God give me patience.

But the questioning went on relentlessly, with the delicacy, Charles Russell thought, of an elephant with arthritic feet.

Then if Russell had kept in touch with Milo his opinion would be valuable in a matter which was troubling them all. That could be put in its simplest form. Who would succeed when Milo died?

'One of the Deputies,' Russell said. It was the answer by the book of words.

'Kamich, for instance?'

'He's much the senior.'

'Of course you know his political leanings.'

'I know he's a man from the Central Province.'

'And Milo's a man of the North.'

'Just so. His wife is from the South. Where are we?'

'Kamich,' Sir Jonathan finally said, 'would hardly be acceptable.'

'No? If he's acceptable to Milo's country I cannot see much you can really do.'

'But would he be acceptable?'

'Tell me. I'm afraid you forget I am now retired.'

The diplomat promptly changed his gear. To Charles Russell the action was almost audible. 'We were hoping for an alternative.'

'Yes?'

'We were wondering about that wife of his.'

'I've often done that. She's a beautiful woman.'

'Do you think that's why he married her?'

'Chiefly.' Charles Russell decided to risk a quotation. ' "Then let thy love be younger than thyself." '

'I beg your pardon?'

'Shakespeare, you know. *Twelfth Night*, Act Two. Also the wisdom of hundreds of harems. And the South of Milo's astonishing country was once a part of the Ottoman empire.'

'She brought him much more than the fact she's younger.'

'She brought him her mother's prestige and name and she's a Member of the People's House. In the South, where she comes from, she had a good deal of influence.'

'And she doesn't lean towards Kamich's politics.'

'You're assuming I know what those are. I suspect.'

'Then you'll realize we'd rather not have him in power.'

'Of course you'd rather not have him in power.'

'Then I'm asking you a simple question. Do you think Milo's wife has a chance of succeeding him?'

'In Milo's country nothing's impossible. She might

succeed him or so might some unknown outsider. That assumes that she wanted to make a fight.'

'And would she?'

'God dammit, Gael Milo's a woman.'

Sir Jonathan rose; he was hiding offence. 'I have troubled you enough,' he said stiffly.

'A pleasure,' Charles Russell said. He was lying.

He went back to his flat with his nerves on edge, despising himself that a cutprice Knight could have ruffled his equanimity. It was early for whisky and soda still but he poured himself a generous drink. He heard his letterbox click and picked out the letter. It bore the badge of Milo's London embassy but when he opened it there was another inside marked *By Favour of Diplomatic Bag*. He slit the second and sat down to read it. In the club they'd been talking of Milo's wife and this was a personal letter from Gael.

He read this letter more than once, an experienced instinct stirring yeastily. Charles Russell could not have achieved what he had if he'd gone solely by the book and logic. His Voices weren't loud and never saintly but when he heard them he listened with real respect. They were telling him now that this formal letter was concealing another message. Distress.

On the face of it there was very little, just a rather conventional note of thanks for hospitality and for great forbearance in a matter the writer needn't mention, plus a renewed and he knew sincere invitation to visit them again in their country. That was all. It was nothing.

It wasn't nothing and Russell sensed it. Milo had thanked him enough for politeness, enough even by Continental standards. Gael might have sent him flowers. She had not. Instead she had sent him this curious letter which contrived to say one thing and mean another. Gael Milo was in serious trouble, Gael Milo wanted Charles Russell's help. She hadn't mentioned her mother, she didn't need to.

He was reasonably sure he wasn't Gael's father but he might well have been if the dates had been different. The affair had been almost as fierce as the fighting but it had left him, as some others had not, with a taste which the years had in no way embittered.

And it wasn't only this letter of hers which was pricking Charles Russell's experienced thumbs. There'd been that look between herself and her husband, a glance which he hadn't been able to read. Lord Tokenhouse, too, hadn't run to form: normally he came clean as a whistle. Lord Tokenhouse had certainly known something but he wasn't prepared to share his knowledge. And what they had learnt about Mid Western was something which didn't make obvious sense. Mid Western might be after Commonwealth but Mid Western had all the iron it could smelt.

... Milo's strange and often still savage country. It was a long way away and by now unfamiliar. One should never go back, it was always a let-down, and his diary was full of amusing engagements.... Gael's mother who'd fought like a man in the mountains but in rare moments of leisure had been wholly a woman. And her daughter was asking for help.

Russell sighed. He wouldn't stay with the Milos with a guest's obligations for he suspected that these might cramp his freedom. After all he was now on Commonwealth's board. There had even been talk, though only in jest, of sending him down to Milo officially. So he mustn't and wouldn't accept hospitality: instead he would stay at a tourists' hotel. Some of them, he had heard, were good.

He picked up the phone and rang his travel agents....

Yes, tomorrow and by a scheduled flight. Not a package tour and a good hotel. The Corals? He had heard well of that one. Tickets at the airport, then? Good. Also the reservation. Better.

He then telephoned to his chairman politely. Lord Tokenhouse had no objection whatever. A change would do Russell a world of good.

Next evening he looked round his hotel bedroom. It was better than he had dared to expect, a little too flash for a delicate taste, but undeniably it was also comfortable. The lighting was good, the bathroom spotless, and the bed was neither too hard nor too soft. The room had a pleasant balcony too, which looked down into a graceful paved courtyard. 'All rooms with sea view'—that was technically true. Not much of the sea might in fact be visible but it was certainly there in the middle distance. Russell had eaten a meal on the aircraft, though his normal habit was not to do so, so he went for a stroll in the well-kept garden and at eleven o'clock he went to bed.

He woke what he guessed was a few hours later, conscious that he was not alone. He had left the balcony door wide open and the moon gave sufficient light to see. Russell looked at the intruder, not moving. If he moved he would probably earn a coshing and discretion was better than ill-timed valour. Besides, he had very little to lose, some traveller's cheques which he hadn't yet cashed and which a common hotel thief might very well leave, a minimum of English money, and a couple of ancient silver-backed brushes which mentally he had written off. Only his grandfather's pocket watch worried him, gold and well worth the immediate taking.

But it wasn't worth risking a probable injury so he lay in a pretended sleep, awaiting events but not for long.

A second man had come into the bedroom.

No, it wasn't a man, it was clearly a woman. She had climbed across the balcony's railing and the balcony was two storeys up. Moreover she wasn't making a sound. This woman, whoever she was, knew her business. She moved silently on rubber-soled shoes. The intruder's back was now turned away from her and she drew a short club and felled him neatly. He collapsed on the floor and she left him there coolly.

Charles Russell sat up and turned the light on. The woman said something he didn't follow.

'Can you speak English?'

She shook her head.

'Understand it a little perhaps?'

The woman didn't answer him. She pointed to a badge on her breast. It said in English since most guests were that: SECURITY. THE CORALS HOTEL.

'You're the hotel dick?'

'I not understand.'

'But you seem to have some words of my language.' He began to speak very slowly indeed, pointing at the man on the floor. 'Who is that one?'

'A villain.'

... She must have been watching English telly.

'What sort of a villain?'

'Please?' she said.

'It doesn't matter. He pointed again. 'What now?' he inquired.

For an answer she picked the hotel thief up. She had a countrywoman's powerful shoulders but she was a very attractive woman indeed. Russell put on a flowered dressing-gown and followed her to the little balcony. He couldn't see a ladder or rope but there was a dangerous-looking drainpipe close. 'To climb up on that was extremely competent, but you won't get him down on your back, you know.'

The girl read his meaning if not the words and she answered with an indifferent smile. She balanced the thief on the cast iron railing, then she gave him a push and he fell two storeys. There was a very uncomforting sound indeed.

Russell looked at her again, impressed. She was heavily built but she wasn't clumsy. She had a very pale skin and raven hair. She reminded him of Gael Milo strongly.

'What happens next?' he asked again.

'Tomorrow,' she said.

'Why not tonight?' He waved at the bedroom door, still open.

'I virgin girl,' the lady said.

'A misfortune which I could happily remedy.'

'Tomorrow,' she said, 'will come a man.'

'It's not the same thing.'

'I not understand.'

'A pity—forget it.'

She put a leg across the balcony's railing, exposing a massive but shapely thigh. 'You're not going to drop,' Russell said. He was horrified. He looked down into the graceful courtyard. 'It must be all of thirty-five feet.'

For answer she swung the other leg over, hanging easily by her hands and laughing. Russell saw that she had magnificent teeth. 'Don't do it,' he said.

'I army girl.' She was evidently proud of it.

'You mean you've been taught to drop and roll?'

The girl didn't answer but hung there smiling. She was thinking this elegant well-preserved Englishman would have been interesting if the rules had allowed it, and she hadn't been telling the literal truth.

'You've been taught how to drop with a parachute?'

'Parachoot?'

He made a gesture above his head, arms curved. The girl nodded; she seemed in no hurry whatever. Her fine bosom rose and fell composedly.

Russell looked down to the courtyard again. He supposed that for people who knew their business the fall wouldn't be worse than a rather bad landing. There was a certain way of rolling quickly, but only a fire and a bad one at that would have tempted him to risk it himself.

'Don't hurt your pretty.'

'I not understand.'

'Your bottom, your buttocks, your nates, your arse.'

'Ass?' the girl asked.

'Not ass, it's arse. Ass is an American transference. I've often wondered how it occurred.'

'Please?'

'Let it pass.' He bent over her, polite and solicitous.

She let go with her right hand and used it to point. She pointed again at the badge on her breast.

'I always here. Mornings not working.'

'That's the best news you've given me.'

The girl smiled and let go. She fell on the balls of her feet, legs bent, then she rolled in a compact professional breakfall. She got back to her feet and she picked up the sneak thief. She slung him across her shoulder and waved.

Charles Russell went back to bed regretfully.

4

With his coffee next morning there was also a note which said in polite, somewhat formal terms that Kamich would do himself the great honour of calling on Colonel Russell that morning. He hoped that ten would not be too early.

Russell received him on his balcony, privately very pleased to meet him. He'd had the inevitable file on Kamich as he'd had on most men with their hands on power's levers, but a record however complete was one thing, the man himself might well be another. Commonwealth would be sinking money here and Kamich was an important man. In the hierarchy he stood second to Milo but second didn't imply subservience. Milo had mellowed since those days in the mountains, he had learnt to bend theory to daily necessity. Charles Russell suspected that Kamich had not—had not and would never wish to. That bore in his club had for once been right. If Kamich succeeded to power in this country the bars would come down again inside and out. Happily Milo, though ageing, seemed vigorous, and his race mostly lived for a very long time.

Russell offered a chair and Kamich took it. Russell placed him in his later forties. He had dark brown hair, beginning to grey, and he wore it very short on his skull. A brachycephalic head and high cheek bones, a peasant's wide shoulders and wider hands. The shoulders might be a peasant's. Not the brain.

For that matter nor was the speech; it was faultless. 'I've come,' Kamich said, 'as a matter of duty. I happened to be in this town on business so it falls to me to call on you first. A privilege.' He bowed and smiled. 'A matter of duty but also a pleasure.'

'You're very kind.'

'I must also apologize. There are people who talk about secret police but Colonel Russell would never use such a term. If he did I should at once protest that in this country today no such thing existed. But I'll admit that there are specialized police and one branch of them is concerned with tourists. You wouldn't believe how stupid some are.'

'I'm afraid that I am one of them. I got myself robbed last night.'

'I know.' Kamich produced Russell's grandfather's watch. 'This is part of my pleasure—to give you this back. The thief will be dealt with when he comes out of hospital.'

'The lady was very efficient.'

'Of course. In this case her duty was to protect you from robbery but she'd be just as decisive on other occasions. We do have some trouble with tourists, you know, though the troublesome ones aren't normally British. But another race gets above itself, insulting people and smashing things up.'

'She looked more than a match for the average kraut.'

'I'm very glad indeed you approve.'

Kamich took the cigar which Russell offered and the two men sat in a comfortable silence. Each was assessing the other quietly. To Kamich Charles Russell was what he'd expected, very English, urbane, entirely reasonable. It would be easy to say what he'd come to convey. Charles Russell was impressed by Kamich though he wasn't a type he would ever admire. This man was what his file had told him, ruthless and a dangerous enemy. Charles Russell would much prefer him as friend and Kamich was flying the signals of amity.

'I introduced myself but we've met before.'

'I'm sorry I don't remember.'

'No?' Kamich began to tell the story which went back to the days in the mountains with Milo. He'd been only a boy with a growing boy's appetite, and though his background had been far from wealthy they'd always had enough to eat. Now they seldom had that and were often starving, and a large part of what had been dropped with Russell wasn't arms—they had mostly captured those— but food and the promise of more to come. But the regular drops had been often disrupted and Kamich had in the end succumbed. He had stolen food from another guerrilla.

It was the unforgivable crime and the penalty death. Charles Russell had thought it by far too severe. In theory he'd been a military adviser though in practice a sort of foreign quartermaster who doled out what the foreigner threw from the skies, but he'd also had access to Milo and Milo appeared to like him. When he'd heard that a boy of sixteen would be shot he had exercised his right to be listened to.

Wasn't it a little extreme to shoot a child for stealing food?

That wasn't the point, they were all men together. Men and the occasional woman. The Major knew what sort of war this was.

Russell had said he was only an Englishman who didn't wish to interfere. Nevertheless such things could happen even in regular British units, but when they did the way they were dealt with was seldom by a firing squad.

Milo replied with a touch of malice that the Major's

most distinguished regiment was hardly if ever in rags and hungry.

That was probably true and Russell was learning; he was learning a different sort of war and the lesson had had much to teach him. Most armies had something to teach the other.

Such as what?

Such as turning a blind eye—an art. If this had happened on active service, he wouldn't pretend it wasn't serious, but the point was the news would never have reached him.

... You mean the men would have dealt with it privately?

Very roughly indeed but they wouldn't have shot him.

We're not regulars here and perhaps mine would.

Which would save you the formalities, wouldn't it?

Milo had laughed and had finally nodded. 'Very well,' he had said, 'let us give it a try.'

Russell had not inquired of the outcome but later he had seen Kamich alive. He'd been heavily bandaged but also living. Russell had forgotten it all but Kamich had not and he never would. As a director of a capitalist firm Charles Russell was fair game to be cheated, but the man who had saved a starving boy's life wasn't one against whom he would lift a finger. Marxist in training and thought and discipline, his private ethos had remained untouched. One avenged a wrong but repaid a benefit and to do anything else would be simply disgraceful. Not all the theory and none of the teachers had scratched what was bred in his stubborn blood.

But he'd come here to warn and began it skilfully. 'One part of my duty was simply to welcome you but another was to offer my thanks.'

'Whatever for?'

'For that affair at your flat.'

'You've heard about that?'

'Of course I have. Our ambassador passed it on at once but naturally we shan't make it public. The local uproar would be extremely awkward and we don't see any advantage whatever.'

'I don't know about the local uproar but I didn't see any advantage either.'

'Another man might have panicked or talked.'

'I didn't see much to be gained by that.'

'And that's why I offer our heartfelt thanks.'

'Would you like a drink?'

'That's very kind.'

Charles Russell rang down for gin and tonic, confident this sophisticate wouldn't thank him for the drink of his country. To order it would be no compliment but simply a rather ingenuous gaffe. When the gin had gone down Russell ordered another. It was time that he asked a few questions himself before the warning which he had sensed was coming.

'May I ask how you knew I was here?'

Kamich stared. 'The question is serious? From Colonel Charles Russell? You know what this country is. We have tourists. Naturally we check on them. Charles Russell is not an unknown name.'

'Then that girl, to whom I'm eternally grateful, had other duties than to prevent a robbery?'

'That is so, though it puts it a little crudely.'

'Perhaps it does but I'm not here officially.'

'If you had been I'd have known of it first.'

'You are delicately warning me? In that case we are almost quarrelling.'

'Which isn't my object. I doubt if it's yours.'

'It isn't—that's why I'm speaking frankly. I'm a director of Commonwealth, which I don't doubt you know, and there are one or two things I might like to look at. With your government's permission, naturally. You'll also know I'm an old friend of Milo's and he invited me here to stay with them. I didn't want to do that, it would have made it official, but I've come down on my own and am paying my bill. If it interests you I am paying it personally. It's not something I'm going to charge to the company.'

Kamich said with his most social smile: 'I think that covers very neatly the motives which it also imputes to me. Some of them I freely acknowledge. So now may I ask when you're calling on Milo?'

'Tomorrow if it turns out convenient. I should hire a car and drive up to the capital.'

'Colonel Russell, you will do no such thing. It's three hours by road and that road is appalling. The train contrives to be even worse.' He tore a page from a pocket book, writing on it and passing it over. 'Ring that number when you've cleared things with Milo. There'll be a light aircraft at your disposal here and of course a car at either end.'

'That is really too kind for a casual visitor.'

'You could never be that even granted you wished it.'

'It's still very kind.'

'It is nothing whatever.'

The promised car was waiting next morning and took Russell to the impressive airport. It was bigger than the one at the capital, the showpiece entry to this tourists' coast. A two-engined propeller aircraft was waiting and it flew low enough to see the country. Charles Russell knew the plane must be climbing since the capital was four thousand feet up, and once away from the coastal strip the tumbled hills began to rise sharply. In the valleys was some sort of cultivation, but there didn't appear to be very much water and Russell knew that this Central Province was poor. Away to the south were the rolling plains, the stamping grounds of Gael Milo's fierce clans, to the north the high mountains where Milo had fought, beyond them again the industrial complex whose earnings, with the tourist traffic, kept this harsh little country from falling apart. That iron might indeed transform its economy—no wonder Milo had come to London. There'd been a time when Milo would rather have starved than risk compromising a grim independence, but experience had blunted suspicion, the sharp edges of dogma had gently eroded. Great riches were buried in barren mountains—why shouldn't his peoples enjoy their fruits?

The plane banked sharply past a wall of rock. In fact it was always a chancy landing, and when a wind blew in from the distant mountains the airport was shut as often as not. But Charles Russell, who knew nothing of flying, only noticed the airport's surprising smallness. There was another car waiting and they drove to the town, to Milo's residence in the central square. It had been the palace of the local governor in the days when this much-fought-over country had been a province of a ramshackle empire. Now it was mostly government offices, the Prime Minister's quarters a modest suite in the wing which looked down on the ancient square.

To Russell's surprise Gael received him alone. He thought she looked tired; she was certainly strained. But evidently she was delighted to see him. 'It was kind of you to come. Milo's ill.'

'Nothing serious, I hope.'

'Yes it is.' She had all of her race's simple directness. 'He looks vigorous and mostly he is. But he's also had three heart attacks.'

'I didn't know that.'

'Hardly anyone does, just myself and the doctors. A few men around him have had to be told—I mean about the previous two—but if it were known he'd had a third I don't see how we'd avoid a crisis.'

'How long do you think you can keep it quiet?'

'Perhaps three days if he gets better quickly, but if he's forced to cancel public appointments everybody will start thinking the worst. He isn't young any more and the doctors can't hide it. No story about a summer cold.'

She was very like her mother, he thought—not a woman to put a disaster obliquely. He had seen that she had been opening letters and had noticed the knife she'd been using to do so. He knew it had been her mother's knife, a formidable and efficient weapon. On the deerhorn handle were five deep notches. Each was a German soldier's life. 'How serious is it in fact?' he asked.

'The next one will almost certainly kill him but nobody knows when that will be.'

She had spoken with her usual calm but Russell could see she was deeply moved. I was right for once, he thought —she loves him. That fool in his club had been wrong as usual: their ages were irrelevant, her ambitions, if she had them still, a matter which she no longer accounted. But she was speaking again with open bitterness. 'Which makes that attempt on his life a nonsense. If they'd guessed he was going to have another they would have waited instead of trying to kill him.'

He risked the question directly. 'And who were the they?'

'Kamich perhaps,' she said at last. 'He could have killed him in London—too dangerous here.'

The thought had occurred to Russell too but the motive was not immediately obvious. 'But he's the natural heir,' he said.

'Maybe. But there's no such thing here as established succession. He's still a hardline communist and he doesn't approve of Milo mellowing. He's bitterly opposed to Commonwealth, though he might let you in and rob you later.'

Charles Russell considered, decided to chance it. 'It was suggested to me the other day that if anything went seriously wrong you might reconsider your own position.'

'Politically?' She wasn't surprised. 'When you meet Milo—I hope in a day or two—I beg you not to put that forward.'

'Why ever not?'

'He'd throw one of his tantrums.'

For the first time that morning they both laughed comfortably. Charles Russell knew about Milo's rages, they'd been as famous as his matchless courage. At first they had come to him perfectly naturally but later, as the legend grew, he had adopted them as part of the act. Twice he'd outfaced famous western statesmen, bawling them into the ground with gusto.

'I'm delighted he's well enough to throw one.'

'It'd do him no good if he threw a real one.'

'Returning to my question though, have you never considered a political comeback. Once they called you the uncrowned queen of the South.'

She answered as she always did, straightly. 'Being Milo's

wife has been more than enough and it's a very long time since I did any fencemending. I'm still a member of the People's House but I very much doubt how many would follow me.'

'In a real crisis it would still be plenty.'

'You think so?'

'I'm sure of it.'

'You're thinking of the army perhaps. That comes from the South and so do I, but that would mean soldiers controlling the country.'

'That depends on who was controlling the soldiers.'

Russell was watching her: the tension had grown. She was sitting immobile, not smoking or fidgeting, but he could see that this beauty was on the rack. He said finally: 'We're sparring—please tell me. You didn't send for me just to talk things over.'

'I sent for you?'

'You asked me to come.'

She didn't deny it. 'Very well, will you help me?'

'I will if I can.'

'It's information I want.'

'If it's something about Commonwealth you'll realize I couldn't possibly tell you.'

'No,' Gael said, 'it's something local.'

'What could I possibly find out locally which you couldn't discover a hundred times faster?'

She began to tell him, relaxing visibly. The tension was there still but easing fast, diminishing in the simple act of sharing a worry with somebody else. Basically something didn't fit, and to anyone with experience of politics that was more scaring than threat of war. Naturally they had done their homework, checking very carefully on Commonwealth. Quite a few of its shares were in Nominees' names but there was nothing so very unusual in that and this holding had been there for years. But there'd recently been a fresh development, somebody new building up an interest. The Commercial Attaché in London was competent.

'You've been thorough,' Charles Russell said.

'Of course. You have to be in a contract of this size.'

Then didn't he feel that it didn't smell right? It couldn't be friends to the east who were buying, that wasn't their form and never had been. If they needed more iron, which she didn't believe, they were much more likely to come in and take it. In any case, buying shares in the market was something they wouldn't do on principle.

'But somebody else might?'

'That's exactly what troubles me.'

'I confess that the thought had occurred to me too but what strangled it was the absence of motive. The people we're both of us thinking of now have more than enough iron ore already, far too much to be tempted to take over Commonwealth.'

She lit a cigarette and inhaled it. 'We've been talking about iron ore,' she said. 'Suppose, just suppose, we were wrong in doing so. Suppose, just suppose, there were something else.'

'What sort of something?'

'I don't know that. I only know that there's something hidden.'

Charles Russell thought it over deliberately. There wasn't an iota of evidence but Gael Milo was not a fanciful woman. He said at last:

'It's a hypothesis but it *would* explain things, certain matters which as you shrewdly say don't otherwise run to normal form. Assuming you're right or partly right who else will have guessed or who else would know?'

'I can't say who's guessed but Milo knows. Your Lord Tokenhouse knows too. Milo told him.'

'You're sure of this?'

'I'm pretty sure.'

'Then why not ask Milo?'

'He might not tell me. There's something and he knows I make guesses, but he doesn't want me involved in politics and I'm not eager to return myself.' She leant forward suddenly, tenser than ever. 'But I would have to if this is what I suspect. When Milo retires there'll be a struggle for power. I might have to go back though God knows how.'

'Does Kamich have suspicions too?'

'I'm inclined to think not, or not just yet. But the man who is trying to use him may. He may even know. They have first-class Intelligence.'

'Bojalian,' Russell said. He was silent. He knew most things about Bojalian for the file on him had been thicker than Kamich's ... Kamich who thought Milo weak, hardline communist who'd never take foreign orders, Kamich who'd called on Colonel Charles Russell. To pay his compliments, to return a watch? No doubt, but there had been something else. Kamich had uttered no overt threat and to Milo's guest he could hardly have done so, but Charles Russell had read the message clearly. He was Milo's old friend, that was quite acceptable, and he was also a director of Commonwealth. That was acceptable too. There it stopped. He mustn't interfere.

He was going to. Gael Milo was cutting him in remorselessly. He sighed but he said again: 'Bojalian.'

'You know about Bojalian?'

'Yes. For the moment we'll gain nothing discussing

him. You were saying you wanted information. Suggest to me, please, where I go to get it.'

'Have you heard of Richard Bentinck?'

'Never.'

'He's a popular and respected consul in the seaside town where you've chosen to lodge. Also he's something very different.'

'He's one of those?'

'Indeed he is. Admittedly I'm guessing now, but suppose there were something up there in those mountains, something besides a lode of iron ore, then there's a motive for someone to buy into Commonwealth, perhaps even to try to take you over.'

'Granted the premise that's perfectly logical. It's also, alas, entirely logical that if the interested parties are those you're implying I'm the last man Richard Bentinck will talk to.'

'You're Colonel Charles Russell,' she said.

'I was. You're sending a boy on a grown man's errand.'

'I don't see it like that.' She looked up. 'You're declining?'

'Frankly, there's little I'd care to refuse you.'

She laughed. 'You're like us. You remember friendships.'

'Then where does this ... er ... consul live?'

'In the old-fashioned quarter down by the port. The bottom of the house is his office. He lives in the flat above. He's not married.' She gave him a card with a telephone number. 'That's personal to me here. You should use it.'

'I'll try,' Charles Russell said, 'to please you. The odds against success are enormous.'

Nevertheless he called that evening after a flight back from the capital which he spent in somewhat uneasy reflection. He was far from convinced that Gael Milo was right, that there was really some mystery locked in her mountains, but he had a logical mind and a lifetime's experience, and it was impressive that if you accepted her guess then several events would form a pattern which, taken alone, were simply untidy. Life was often like that, especially privately, but politics usually ran to form, most notably those of communist States. If Richard Bentinck received him and talked of nothing then the inference, though not conclusive, was clear: Gael Milo was very probably wrong. But if Bentinck should send him packing brusquely then the chances were he had something to hide. That wouldn't give Russell information but it would put him upon a line to obtain it.

The office was shut: Russell rang the flat bell. Richard Bentinck appeared and Russell gave him his card. Bentinck was startled and didn't hide it. 'Colonel Russell,' he said in his Ivy League accent, 'I'm very greatly honoured indeed. I'm also very gravely embarrassed.'

'I can think why.'

'That I can't ask you in.'

'Why ever not?'

'You're Colonel Charles Russell.'

'I happen to be what you call a Bird Colonel and I don't conceal that my name is Russell. I also happen to be retired.'

'Some men never retire.'

'I have.'

'I doubt it.' Bentinck looked at Charles Russell with open resentment. 'I suppose it didn't occur to you that you've probably been followed here.'

'But of course it did. I have. I noticed him. Two of them, I rather fancy.'

'Then aren't you taking a foolish risk?'

'That depends.'

'On what?'

'On what you may decide to tell me.'

'Colonel Russell, I have nothing to tell you. I have nothing to tell you of any kind.'

'I'm sorry,' Charles Russell said. He turned. He went back to the Corals and went quietly to bed. He had liked the look of Richard Bentinck but he hadn't been impressed by his manner. He was the middle-piece agent, still young and still learning. And why should Richard Bentinck be otherwise? This country wasn't worth a flyer and if something blew up they could always send one. But inconsiderable as a serious agent he'd be a very good ally indeed in trouble. Russell knew the type well, they'd been trained and were dedicated.

Richard Bentinck went down to his favourite bar where he was something more than merely accepted; he was welcome by now, almost one of the boys. The local opinion of Richard Bentinck was that he was that rarest of international animals, the American who drank in a civilized way. He took two or three drinks but he never got drunk, he chatted fluently with working sailors, he never went rude or broke the glasses and, incredible to these simple folk who had fixed ideas about all Americans, he never got maudlin and wept on your shoulder. He wanted to be loved? He did not. He just wanted to be accepted. He was.

He took his ration of drink and then went to his bed, waking to a strong smell of smoke and the ominous crackle of powerful flame. He tried to jump from the bed and found that he couldn't. He was conscious, his mind was as clear as a bell, but he was paralysed below the waist. He rolled from the bed to the floor and lay there. Now his arms had gone too, he was finally helpless. On the floor the smoke was thickening steadily, the noise of the flames had increased to a roar.

Oh God, he thought, what a way to die.

5

Kamich had realized a crisis was imminent but he hadn't expected the way it would come. It arrived with an open call from Bojalian which was something very unusual indeed. Bojalian preferred to work in the shadows.

Kamich had always intensely disliked him both for what stood behind him and what he was. Officially he was another Bentinck, a man with a post in his country's embassy but in practice holding one much more important, and his country was at the opposite pole from Bentinck's powerful but often clumsy giant. It was the country which Kamich had always most feared, the reason why his private thinking was uncomfortably split between Kamich the communist and Kamich the man who would fight without question if his native independence were threatened. And Bojalian's country could do just that. They didn't think as Americans did, hamstrung by ancestral naggings about a world which was free but also innocent: on the contrary they thought in terms of *Realpolitik*. They might rather see Kamich as Premier than Milo but if he got there they wouldn't change their policy. That would remain what it always had been, that Milo's country was a difficult neighbour, one which wanted it both ways, East and West. Step over a line which was never defined and you wouldn't last long to regret the error.

Bojalian had arrived in a fury and Kamich's dislike of

him rose. Bojalian was an Armenian, a race which had suffered most forms of oppression, but now that he had power behind him the inevitable had inevitably happened. Bojalian threw his weight about, Bojalian was a shocking bully. Kamich who'd won his freedom by fighting hated this man and resented his manner.

He had come storming in and had banged the table. 'You must act at once,' he had said. 'Immediately. If you do not I cannot control the consequences.'

'Act about what?'

'This man Charles Russell.'

'I know all about the Colonel Russell. He's here at Milo's invitation, though he didn't elect to stay under their roof. He's also a director of Commonwealth, but I'm capable of dealing with Commonwealth. Russell's politically unimportant since his country is now a weak-kneed sham. It gets smugger and more impotent daily.'

'Did you know that he'd called on Bentinck?'

'Yes.' Kamich sat upright. 'And how did you?'

'By the same means you employed yourself. I put a man on his tail to report his movements.'

'That's a very irregular thing to do. We know what you are but this isn't your country.'

'Try complaining to my embassy, then.' Bojalian was being aggressive.

'I don't propose to waste my time.' Kamich considered the man before him; he loathed bullies but it was seldom true that bullying was a cloak for cowardice. This man was an abrasive boor but his record was one of effective action. For the moment Kamich swallowed his anger. 'May I know why you had Colonel Russell followed?'

'Because we're a cautious and thorough people.' He made what for Bojalian was almost a gesture of friendly

compromise. 'But possibly you're right about Russell—
alone he could hardly upset your plans. But when he goes
to see Bentinck——'

'They talked on the doorstep.'

'Then Bentinck has something to hide.'

'It's conceivable.'

'Bentinck is playing a hand of his own, or at any rate
he is for the moment. But sooner or later he'll gang up
with Russell.'

'Then why was he handing him off?'

'He's not ready. He's waiting for orders from you know
where. Perhaps they haven't yet cleared their position.
It's the only safe assumption.'

'Why?'

'Because, my friend, my masters think so.'

'God damn your great blundering bureaucrat masters.'

'Unhappily for you they have power. More unhappily
I am also their agent.' Bojalian was enjoying it brutally.

Kamich forced himself back to a cold control. 'If Bentinck is playing a hand of his own why should you or
your masters fear it? While I'm alive he won't get that
iron.'

Bojalian lit a grey cigar. The tobacco was Caucasian
where, Kamich thought, they made lovely rugs but also
grew the world's worst tobacco. He didn't offer a smoke
to Kamich. For the moment his bullying manner had
blunted: in its place he was pompously self-important.
'There is something I must tell you now. Before I didn't
have the authority but I signalled last night and now I
have. We've been talking about iron ore.'

'We have.'

'In which, as it happens, I've little interest.'

'Then why have you called?'

'There is something else.'

'Something else besides iron up there in the mountains?'

'So we're informed and we don't make mistakes.'

'What is it, then?'

Bojalian told him in a single short word. It had driven some men to stupendous effort, others very close to madness. It had a place in mythology, another in politics. Beautiful women were offered it ritually. All men desired and few possessed it.

Bojalian rose with a dangerous smile. He could see that Kamich was badly shaken. Let him put that in his pipe and smoke it, not fine tobacco he wouldn't appreciate.

Kamich seldom drank except purely socially but now he poured brandy and drank it fast. Sensational was an overworked word but it was also the one most men would use. So it was futile to think of letting in Commonwealth, then picking some quarrel and seizing their assets. What he'd been told had altered that. Once in he'd never get them out, they'd have allies or could readily find them. They would for what was up there in the mountains. The children of every race oppressed were born with a lie on their ready lips but Kamich could think of no possible motive for Bojalian telling a lie in this case. It was there all right and Milo must know it. How Bojalian did was not yet relevant. Some spy, Kamich thought. They had very efficient ones.

Another thought struck him, even more scaring. Bojalian's masters would want this too, they'd want it very badly indeed. Their next move would be to demand a concession and if they didn't get that they might do anything. No question with them of discreet intervention on behalf of some company's assets abroad. They'd never worked like that and they never would. They'd come in; they were realists.

Kamich poured himself a second drink. What he needed was time and he'd have to make it, time to consider his country's position, his own if it came to that and it did.... Charles Russell—no, he wasn't yet dangerous. Such evidence as there was suggested that the old fox had somehow become suspicious, so he'd gone to Dick Bentinck for confirmation. If he'd *known* he'd have acted at much higher levels, he needn't have come to the country at all. And Bentinck had sent him firmly packing, Richard Bentinck was playing his cards alone.

Of course he was, and a powerful collection. His country was a powerful country.

Time, Kamich thought again—time to plan. Eliminating Richard Bentinck would do nothing to solve his longterm problem, nothing to release his country from the two opposite grindstones which threatened to crush it. What stood behind Bentinck could soon replace him, but for a vital few days there'd be room to breathe. So cut their communications quickly for without information they'd hardly dare act. Of course it would have to look like an accident, though Bentinck's employers would guess it was not.

He summoned and spoke to two men he trusted. Richard Bentinck had accepted his risks.

For a moment his native mistrust of all foreigners flared up into almost personal hatred. Americans caused trouble everywhere, Americans should stay quietly at home. If they didn't they simply bought what they asked for.

The barman hadn't liked it a bit, Richard Bentinck spent freely and moreover was popular, but he knew

68

which side his bread was buttered. If he refused they'd shut him down in a week and the man with the drug had been reassuring. There wouldn't be any embarrassment locally, no collapse on the barman's respectable premises; this drug was a slow-acting one and Bentinck would go home quietly as usual. So put it in one of his drinks and Serve the State. The barman hadn't dared to decline and in any case hadn't considered a killing. He knew Bentinck was a United States consul who lived above his place of work and he assumed there was going to be, well, some check on it. This drug would put Bentinck out while they did it. When he woke he would be more than suspicious, he might even stop using his favourite bar. Too bad—he was liked there as well as respected. But the loss of a single customer was much better than having the business shut down.

The barman had done it since he couldn't do otherwise and Bentinck was lying and waiting to die. He was hoping that Death wouldn't drag his feet for he hadn't much more which he dared to hope for. The smoke had already begun to choke him, and though he could barely move his head he could see that the flames were creeping closer.

Charles Russell was conscious too and restless, though for reasons which were entirely different. Normally he could sleep like a child but his talk with Gael had disturbed him deeply, and it hadn't been agreeable that Richard Bentinck had in effect dismissed him. He was lying for once courting sleep unsuccessfully, and when the fire engine banged its bell in the street he decided that a walk in the night might possibly give the relief he needed.

Another engine went by as he put on his clothes, and once in the street he could see the fire's glow. It was somewhere down towards the harbour and Russell began to trot there quickly. When he came to the water he stood and stared. It was the house where a matter of hours ago Richard Bentinck had declined to talk to him.

The old building was burning hard and noisily and a part of the roof had already gone. On the quay there were several fire tenders, brightly painted and modern and clearly efficient, machines to impress the foreign tourist. They were efficient but not behaving efficiently, spraying the buildings on either side and certainly stopping the fire from spreading, but apparently someone had quietly decided that the house itself was past all saving. Charles Russell had seen a good many fires and some of them he had known to be arson. A familiar suspicion stirred, but uncertainly. The crews were working, well drilled and disciplined, but they were leaving Dick Bentinck's house to burn. And it *was* a house, not merely an office. At the top was the flat where Dick Bentinck lived.

Someone plucked at his sleeve and he turned at once. It was the security girl from the Corals hotel and she said something which he didn't follow. She was looking at the fire and frowning.

Russell tried her in Italian though on this coast that was a dangerous language. People had gone to prison and worse on no more than suspicion of speaking Italian. 'Incendio,' he said, and waited.

To his relief she answered him, thickly but she was still intelligible. 'A bad one,' she said.

'I can see that too. Why don't they try to put it out?'

'They're trying to save the other houses.'

'It's not only an office, you know. Someone lives there.'

'The American consul is not at home.'

'But how do you know?'

'I asked the captain and he told me it's empty.'

'And did you believe him?'

She didn't reply but moved her shoulders. 'I killed a man once,' she said. 'With my hands. He was an Enemy of the People. A Duty.' The capitals came across loud and clear.

'But you've never burnt a man at the stake?'

'*Scusi?*'

'You wouldn't burn a man alive.'

She had lighted a cigarette but now dropped it. 'Burning is very bad,' she said. 'The Germans brought petrol and burnt my grandfather. They tied up my mother and made her watch.' She looked at the fire again and shivered. 'Would you come with me?' she asked.

'Since I must.' Charles Russell was scared and not ashamed of it.

She took his hand; then began to run. Somebody shouted, then roared an order. Two firemen in helmets blocked their way. One moment they were standing upright, the next they were flat on the ground and writhing. The girl had hardly seemed to move. 'I've been here before,' she said, 'on business. There's a fire escape at the back, in the garden.'

They were in it now, but halted uncertainly. Russell looked at the increasing inferno: whoever had started this fire knew his business. The fire escape was still erect but it wasn't too clear what was holding it up. At the bottom the wall was already crumbling, stones scattered across the narrow path which ran between wall and Dick Bentinck's swimming-pool. Where the fire escape met the narrow path the stanchions had been concreted in. It was this which was holding it up. Nothing else.

'That won't take us both,' she said.

'I'll go.'

'I'm lighter than you are.' She was speaking her rough Italian still.

'I started this.'

He pushed her; it was a grave mistake. Again he hardly saw her move, but in the swimming-pool he was swimming crossly. He heard her laugh once and that was all. By the time he got his respected head up she was half-way up the tottering ladder. She stopped and called down through the darkening smoke.

'You stay where you are. Don't move. Just wait.'

Charles Russell obeyed: he had guessed her plan. No heroics from him, he thought, God damn her. It was humiliating but it was also sensible. In action he'd only have got in her way.

He watched her on the fire escape anxiously. The angle irons which supported the ladder, clamped to the wall at four-foot intervals, had broken away from the weakened masonry. It was held by its feet in the concreted path and the higher she went the more it swayed. Once he thought it had gone but it somehow held. Her hands had reached a window-sill now. The glass had already splintered outwards.

The fire escape fell and buckled wickedly. The girl pulled herself up and disappeared. Charles Russell heard his own voice briefly. It seemed to be saying a stumbling prayer.

He had counted thirty-one unknowingly when the girl reappeared at the broken window. Her face had been blackened by smoke and grime and her blouse hung about her in ragged tatters. If she'd been burnt she was hiding it stoically. She called down to Russell, still swimming and waiting.

'Which is the deep part?'

'This one. The nearer.'

'How deep is it?'

'About six feet.' He corrected himself. 'Rather under two metres.'

For a moment she disappeared again but only to bend her powerful back. She came up with Bentinck's head, then his shoulders, balancing him on the broken window-sill. 'He's been drugged,' she said. 'I'll have to throw him. Don't try to catch him, just keep out of the way.'

She picked up the paralysed man and called down again.

'Ready?'

'Aye, ready.'

She threw him in a wide parabola.

... That's the second time she's done that. She's good at it.

There was an enormous splash but a perfectly clean one. The girl had thrown Bentinck well clear of the parapet.

'Get him down to the shallow end.'

Russell did so.

There was another splash, this time much tidier. Russell was holding Bentinck's head. He seemed to be conscious, his eyes were moving. His lips formed words but no words came.

A knot of men had run round to the garden, standing by the swimming-pool tensely. One of them said:

'I'm a doctor.'

'Good.'

They pulled Bentinck from the shallow end but Russell climbed out by the ladder unaided. The doctor bent over Richard Bentinck and Russell looked round for the girl.

She had gone.

6

Gael Milo's guess had been perfectly right: Milo had told Lord Tokenhouse what his mountains held besides iron ore. There was gold and perhaps a great deal of it, a new Reef, a new Rand, potentially a new Johannesburg. Which was the reason he had come to Commonwealth. He wouldn't pretend he loved them like brothers but they were the best of the field he was forced to choose from. Milo couldn't raise the enormous sums which would be needed to handle a revolution (and that was what it was going to be, a revolution in international finance and liquidity) but at least he could see that the cream of the benefits came squarely back to his own lean country. He wouldn't let history repeat itself blindly; he wouldn't be another Kruger, his country in pawn to detested *uitlanders*. He was offering Commonwealth rights of extraction and he hadn't a doubt they'd prove highly profitable. If they tried to move beyond that limit he would break them and he believed he could. But with some other House backed by a stronger Power his position would be much less secure. That was why he had come to London, not another country with far more money but also far more at stake from a new source of gold. Lord Tokenhouse understood him? Excellent.

Lord Tokenhouse had indeed understood him for he had taken a solid liking to Milo. They were men from very different backgrounds but they had one thing in common and that was important. Both had been bred to the art of politics; each recognized that in the other and trusted it.

The news had astonished the chairman of Commonwealth but it hadn't dismayed him or thrown him off stride. The first emotion of any economist would probably have been to panic—one part of his world would be shaken violently—but Lord Tokenhouse was no sort of economist, indeed he despised the whole ragbag wholeheartedly He sat on more boards than Commonwealth Mining and on each had made his opinion clear: young men with degrees in economics were not to be employed in his companies, and if one from the L.S.E. had slipped in he should be quietly got rid of as soon as possible. Pure economics might sometimes be useful, but diluted with something called sociology they were a menace to well-conducted business. Nevertheless he was far from pig-headed and since gold was in question he had better inform himself. He had bought a book and had read it carefully.

It hadn't told him very much, or not much that he hadn't already guessed. Everyone knew that gold production was much less than was needed to carry trade, and all that this ill-written opus had given him were some figures to support that knowledge. It appeared that in the last four years gold production outside the Soviet bloc had been some eight hundred millions of dollars a year. Half of that went into private hoards or was taken by industrial users, which meant, when you'd fought through the costive prose, that the increase for national reserves was inadequate, a mere one-point-three per cent a year and rather unlikely to rise in the future. There were respectable economists who believed that the answer was funny money, something issued by the I.M.F., and of course there was a vocal left wing which insisted that this new liquidity must be earmarked for those who needed it most, what were deceptively called the emergent States. And there were other and rather more orthodox pundits with an answer which was a good deal simpler. Why not simply raise the price of gold?

Lord Tokenhouse had laughed aloud. Since this tedious book had been tediously written that, in effect, was what had happened. The official price was now thirty-eight dollars but that could hardly hold for long. The dollar was inconvertible, or convertible only in special circumstances, and the free price of gold was rising steadily.... Admit the position and tidy it up by a straightforward honest devaluation? Good heavens no, that wasn't acceptable. Angry talk about a dollarette could embarrass no less than a reigning President, and in any case who stood to gain? The holders of the largest reserves and naturally the gold producers. The two biggest of these were both mistrusted though for reasons which were diametrically different. It simply wasn't on politically to hand them out an enormous bonus.

So Lord Tokenhouse had done his homework but it wasn't the figures which most impressed him, far less the fog of abstract theory. It had been the reference, which had struck him as innocent, to production outside the Soviet bloc. It was production inside which was really the joker, since gold, to any right-thinking communist, would never be a mere commodity nor purely a means of buying abroad what his country very sorely needed. It would be a political weapon to be used politically, as France, to her own economic loss, had used her gold to avenge herself for Anglo-Saxon affronts which were partly imagined.

Milo's country was very dangerously placed.

Lord Tokenhouse saw the problem politically, not as one which might affect the lives of races to whom he was coolly indifferent. Milo had pressed him for temporary secrecy: if possible even his board shouldn't hear till circumstances made the telling necessary. Lord Tokenhouse thought it perfectly possible—Macrae the accountant, solid and Scots, who would see it at once in terms of hard profits, and Weston who was very much cleverer but who also sat on other boards and had a brother who was the company's broker. Never expose a man to temptation. Nor would he wish to tell Shaw, the expert, who'd behaved as an expert so often did, looking for what he expected to find, blind to all else which those mountains might hold. Shaw would lose face, might insist on checking, and that would suit neither Milo nor Tokenhouse. There was only one man whom he trusted to help him and he had gone down to Milo's country, to a holiday hotel by the sea. If he chose to do that he was perfectly free to, and Charles Russell had friends there so why not visit them? But Tokenhouse needed to talk to him urgently. He could talk to him in a common language, the language of the starkest reality.

He wrote out, and sent, an immediate telegram. He'd be very much more than merely grateful for Charles Russell's return for consultation.

It was an irony which Lord Tokenhouse savoured that the only man who had so far approached him had had the politics of it right by accident though he hadn't even mentioned gold. It had been that ass from the club, Sir Jonathan Something, and how anybody quite so pompous could have climbed near the top of an ancient profession was explicable only by sharply reminding oneself that that profession had been cut to pieces. The cry was now equal chances for all. When Tokenhouse had been rather younger a man like this Sir Jonathan Something would have ended his service decoding telegrams. The thought amused Lord Tokenhouse but it didn't increase his reserve of patience. That had never been very notable and the Sir Jonathans could exhaust it rapidly.

He could have rung and suggested a drink at the club, an invitation which Lord Tokenhouse would have found difficult to refuse but might have, but instead he had written a formal letter leaving him with no option whatever. Lord Tokenhouse's distaste for pomposity was now reinforced by something acuter. Lord Tokenhouse felt a real resentment and little or no obligation to hide it.

... The Foreign Office had certain sources, sources of worldwide information.

Lord Tokenhouse didn't answer this. He knew that these sources were second-rate and that men to whom information was vital went somewhere very different to get it.

... And these sources had come up with a story, that there was iron in Milo's most critical country and that Commonwealth might be taking an interest.

'I can confirm that and do but it's very old hat. The *Financial Times* has already speculated.'

Any normal man would have seen he'd been snubbed but Sir Jonathan was not abashed. He had also heard another story, that an American firm was interested too.

'That could be true though I've not been approached.'

... Then might Sir Jonathan know the chairman's feelings in the event that approach should ever be made?

'That's a totally hypothetical question. I might also suggest that it's grossly improper.'

Sir Jonathan became very serious, which in his case

meant more pompous than ever. Iron ore was a matter of great importance, not only to Britain but to all of the West. The Swedish source was strategically vulnerable and no man dared guess what the Swedes would do if serious pressure were brought to bear on them.

Lord Tokenhouse had nodded. He knew it.

Sir Jonathan went all diplomatic. On the stage it would have been overacting, the caricature of a low comedy diplomat. He talked round the subject, he huffed and puffed; and he drove Tokenhouse close to an open explosion. Nevertheless the message came over. In the ordinary language of ordinary men the facts were there and all were connected. First, this iron ore was extremely important. Secondly, Britain was no longer powerful (Sir Jonathan took six minutes to say it since it was something which implied his own impotence). It followed that in the highest circles, a phrase which had made Lord Tokenhouse writhe, there was a feeling that a more powerful ally would be a matter to their mutual advantage. For once there would be little resistance if the Americans cut in on this one: on the contrary there would be much relief.

When Sir Jonathan had taken his leave Lord Tokenhouse sat down and smiled. He had a very sharp taste in irony and it struck him as superbly ironical that Sir Jonathan had been talking of iron. If he'd known it was gold he wouldn't have wuffled; he'd have arrived in a sweat and an open panic. It was amusing that for once he'd been right, much more so than the idiot knew. That was politics and ineluctable. It was also too serious to leave to diplomacy.

Lord Tokenhouse weighed it up very carefully. Someone was building a stake in his company and it was a very fair guess at the builder's identity. So far he'd garnered twenty per cent, powerful but still short of decisive. Another twelve per cent would in practice be that and twelve per cent was in Nominees' names, a merchant bank's creatures and a very respectable one. But Lord Tokenhouse knew what his board did not; he knew the name of the beneficial owner. That knowledge he kept to himself quite properly for he wasn't one of the lady's trustees and as such not the legal owner of shares which if he had been he'd have declared to his company.

He picked up a phone and rang a cousin. 'Auntie Mabel,' he said. 'You're still a trustee.'

'The doctors give her a week at most.'

'Have you seen her?'

'No. They keep her sedated.'

'A fair innings,' Lord Tokenhouse said. 'Ninety-one.'

'I've sent her flowers.'

'And so shall I.'

Kamich had seen it as clearly as Tokenhouse but from a very different point of view. He wasn't concerned with gold as a weapon, something which could be used between nations almost as destructively as a blast from the latest nuclear horror; he thought more simply than that but just as validly. Gold was different from iron but the same in principle. It was his country's gold and nobody's else's. No other must benefit, no other should.

He realized that end would be far from easy. He was the senior of three Deputy Prime Ministers, but Milo, Old Master, had told him nothing. That didn't surprise him for Milo was cagey. Kamich thought Milo had now gone soft but Milo suspected that Kamich's leanings were strongly towards another country. This was perfectly true as political theory, Kamich was still an orthodox communist, but Milo had never quite accepted that at bottom

Kamich was patriot first. In any sort of political crisis Kamich would think of his own country first and all others could go to their various hells; he'd put his country first as Milo had not. Milo had sold out to the British.

And Bojalian had alas been right. Charles Russell, at this moment in time, was probably not an active menace, but when Bentinck was ready they'd strike an alliance. When Commonwealth would have power behind them, real power, not some British consensus government. Americans might not think politically but would do most things to make and keep a dollar. The first was their weakness, the second their strength. If Commonwealth now came in at all Kamich would never get them out.

He frowned for he knew the worst had happened. He had always feared that events would drive him, forcing him into decisions and actions which were convenient neither in time nor circumstance.

He understood his own country perfectly. On the surface it was western, civilized, but underneath it was a boiling brew of races which had never fused. Any fool could start a civil war but only a very great fool would do so, since a civil war could mean intervention and however much you might hate your neighbour you hated any foreigner worse. That was one thing which Milo had always clung to, even as he'd grown older and softer. Somehow he'd held them all together.

Then go on the air and tell the truth, that their mountains were full of uncounted gold and that Milo had let in a stranger to work it? He mightn't last long after that: nor would Kamich. Bojalian knew and so did his masters. Force their hands like that and they'd act at once. Blowing the story prematurely would be an invitation to what he most feared. This was his tightrope and he'd have to walk carefully.

He put his longterm problem aside with relief for he had others which he considered more pressing. Bojalian had been ringing angrily but so far he had declined to receive him. He couldn't do that for very much longer. If the Power which stood behind Bojalian lost patience and pulled the trigger first then there wouldn't be any sort of question of trying to walk the tightrope he hoped to. He wouldn't get even a single foot on it, he'd be up in the hills again, hopelessly fighting, though this time against a different enemy.

Meanwhile there were matters demanding attention, specifically Richard Bentinck and Russell. Russell had rescued Bentinck from death but Kamich didn't believe he had had foreknowledge. If the plan had been leaked before they had met then Russell would have warned Dick Bentinck, who wouldn't have gone home to be burnt but would have spent the night in his island cottage; and if the leak had come after their meeting, Russell would hardly have gone out alone, teaming up with some woman not yet identified. By all accounts it had sounded like Magda, but Kamich did not intend to punish her. She hadn't been privy to what he'd intended and she was far too good an operator to leave rotting in some secret prison.

He decided that Russell was not yet dangerous; he had a day or two to deal with Russell. He'd been poking about after a warning not to, but Kamich didn't believe he had got very far. He would, though, once he'd teamed up with Bentinck. He was a member of the Board of Commonwealth and moreover he had access to Milo. Potentially he was most dangerous of all.

Happily he needn't be killed. Kamich knew a gentler

way and was confident he could use it effectively. He'd go to the British ambassador, explaining that a man like Charles Russell, lately head of the Security Executive, was, well, not exactly *persona non grata*, but evidently a local embarrassment. He'd be obliged to bait the hook a bit with some story which was not the true one, but he knew all about the British ambassador. His Excellency wouldn't bother to check even if he had wished to do so; he'd do anything for smooth relations, do any man to keep his own nose clean. So a telegram would go back to the Foreign Office and thereafter the Whitehall wheels would move greasily. Charles Russell was by now retired but he was also a retired civil servant. Kamich knew perfectly how that world worked. He reckoned it would take three days.

But Bentinck was something entirely different, Bentinck was still an immediate danger. It was too risky to try to kill him again. Once could have been an accident, though Bentinck would certainly know it had not been, but twice would be something more than coincidence. There would probably be some form of protest, which Kamich, as Foreign Minister, would refute with official indignation, but there might also be some form of action and he couldn't foresee what that action might be. It would be dangerous to invite irritation, as dangerous with the West as the East. Anything might result. He was hooked.

Nevertheless if he couldn't now kill him he must somehow be securely neutralized. That cottage of Bentinck's —now that might do. Normally he used it only for fishing, but now, since he had nowhere else, he was camping there and using the ferry. That cottage was on the Isle of Eels.

He sent for a doctor, a sound Party man, and when he arrived offered a good plum brandy. 'Those cholera cases, they're very embarrassing.'

83

'For the tourist trade, you mean? Indeed. But so far we've managed to keep it quiet.'

'How many are there?'

'Four more today.'

'Making forty in all?'

'I'm afraid that's so.'

'How long can you hold it?'

'I can't tell you that.'

'Where are you keeping them?'

'Outside the town.' The doctor smiled a good Party man's smile. 'The new hospital is very impressive. An excellent investment, Minister. Foreigners pay me many compliments.'

'They wouldn't if they knew the truth.'

'You mean that in a separate wing are forty cholera patients, some of them dying? Unfortunately there's no Isolation. You'll remember that we talked of it once but the expense was considered too great to justify.'

'There used to be one,' Kamich said.

'You mean the old one on the Isle of Eels? It hasn't been used for nearly three years.'

'Is it derelict?'

'It's far from that. It's good enough to die in, anyway.'

'I don't think we can accept this risk. The tourist trade could dry up like a tap.' Kamich added on a note of reflection: 'Lucky we didn't build that hotel.'

'On the island, you mean?'

'I mean on the island. What is there now, by the way? Who lives there?'

'There's a handful of brokendown fishermen's cottages, but only one or two are inhabited. One belongs to the local American consul.'

'Very well,' Kamich said, 'move your forty out there.

84

Take the minimum staff and make sure they're secure.'

'Pointless unless you cut the ferry.'

'I fully intend to cut the ferry.'

'And you'll need some form of waterguard if you really want an Isolation.'

'That can be arranged and will be.'

'No doubt you realize the disadvantages—to me and to my staff and the patients.'

'We can't go on taking this risk any longer. If the truth gets out then the Season is finished. Tourists mean money. We need it badly.'

'Very well, then.' The doctor rose. 'One difficulty—it's the American consul.'

'Whose house was burnt down and now sleeps on the island? Too bad on the American consul.'

'We don't warn him?'

'He's an unlucky man.'

7

Charles Russell had read his chairman's telegram, then he put it in an inside pocket. Lord Tokenhouse could wait for a while. Russell had other game to hunt and the scent of it was now strong in his nostrils. He must make Bentinck talk and he now had a weapon. Put at its crudest they'd saved the man's life.

It had been simple to find where Bentinck was lodging. Russell had rung to the wreck of the consulate and the operator had transferred the call. A clerk had answered politely and openly. Yes, this was the consul's temporary office, and no, he wasn't there at the moment. He hadn't in fact come in that morning but if the matter was an urgent one he had a cottage on the Isle of Eels. It didn't have a telephone but there was a public ferry which left from the harbour.

To his surprise Russell found that it wasn't working. It was there all right, still moored to the jetty, but there wasn't a sign of the captain or crew. He tried a bystander in English, who shrugged; there was a notice board but he couldn't read it. Finally he walked down to the beach. There was a longshoreman here with a few words of English and Charles Russell advanced a proposition. He wanted to go to the Isle of Eels and would pay a fair price for a private passage. The longshoreman knew it was now out of bounds but he was poor and he was also cunning. There were armed police on the Isle of Eels at this moment and he didn't propose to risk their fire. But he would take this mad Englishman half-way over and when a warning shot came across his bows he'd turn round and simply bring him back. Half of any fare agreed he'd insist on being paid in advance. He asked for ten pounds in English money. Russell said two and they settled for four. Russell passed over two one-pound notes.

He climbed into the dinghy warily and the longshoreman started the ancient motor. The island was maybe a mile and a quarter and the smooth sea shone in the warm bland sun. Behind them beyond the port were the beaches, and Charles Russell knew that even so early, ten o'clock on a superlative morning, they'd be filling fast with the sun's fierce subjects. A lovely day for sunbathing, assuming, that is, that the bug had bitten you. Russell himself had never succumbed.

He fell into a contented doze to be awakened by the sound of shouting. A launch had put out from the Isle of Eels and a man in the bows had a powerful loudhailer. The longshoreman shouted something back. At the same time he put the tiller down hard.

'What was that?'

'We no go.'

'Why ever not?'

'Island now government. Not to go there.'

Charles Russell was very annoyed indeed. He had parted with money which he wouldn't see back and he suspected some officious muddle. These were coastguards or sailors out on an exercise, pretending the affair was a secret. He looked at the launch again and froze; he had seen what he hadn't seen the first time, a second man in the bows lying prone with a rifle. At the same time he saw a third swimming strongly.

The rifleman raised his rifle and fired. The first of his shots missed the swimmer by yards, but the second splashed very close to his head. The swimmer at once disappeared in a dive.

When Richard Bentinck had first heard the news he had taken it rather less than seriously. He had heard it from one of the neighbouring fishermen whose livelihood had been summarily ended when he couldn't take his catch to the mainland. Bentinck had been sorry for him, but he hadn't supposed that this sudden order would be blindly applied to a foreign official. He had legitimate daily work to do, and once he had got away from the island they might very well stop him coming back. That would be inconvenient since he'd have to find a place to sleep, but it wouldn't be more than a tiresome nuisance. The public ferry was now immobilized but Bentinck had come in his motorized tender. He had breakfast and walked down to it leisurely. The sun was shining, it was going to be hot. There were a great many things though not always the right ones to be said for this extraordinary country. They drugged your whisky and then tried to burn you, but when a man and a girl appeared and saved you they'd in no way interfered with the rescue. Later they'd carried you off to hospital where they'd pumped out your stomach with cool efficiency, explaining you'd taken one over the eight and had set fire to your bed with a cigarette. Bentinck never smoked in bed but no matter.

Which reminded him of another reason for reaching the mainland this shining morning. He must pay an urgent call on Charles Russell. The drug had paralysed his power of movement but not blinded him and he'd recognized Russell. Now he had to contact him, not only to thank him for services rendered but also to tidy up several loose ends. It was Bentinck who now wanted information and he might have to pay in the coin he'd refused. Very well, that would be fair exchange.

He approached his boat in a mood of euphoria which collapsed as he saw an armed man guarding it. As Bentinck came nearer he drew his gun. Bentinck who spoke the language said angrily:

'What's going on?'

'The island is in isolation. Nobody may come here or leave.'

'I'm the American consul.'

'Those are my orders.

Bentinck could see that the man meant business but he was still inclined to believe in mistake in a country where over-zeal was endemic. He walked crossly to the tiny shop, the only telephone on the Isle of Eels. He'd put a call through to the capital, to a man he knew well in Foreign Affairs, and if that didn't work he'd ring his embassy.

The shopkeeper very much regretted but no calls to the mainland were being accepted.

Richard Bentinck began to take it seriously, there was too much here for a simple mistake. It was the timing which worried him more than the facts. An attempt to murder him had been one thing, part of the risks of his curious trade, but he knew that it wouldn't be made without motive and that motive would have to be sudden and urgent. Charles Russell could maybe throw light on that, and when an attempt on his life was promptly followed by a decision which would in effect imprison him there was all the more reason to talk to Russell.

He went back to his cottage and changed into bathing trunks. He would look a proper jerk, he thought, driving up through the town in no more than a slip in his car which he had parked by the jetty, and in any case such an act was illegal. But he knew the back alleys, should reach his new office, and there he had an efficient clerk who would find him clothes and make him respectable. He was a very strong swimmer; he'd make it easily.

He didn't go to the beach where he kept his tender, but slipped out of the back door of the cottage, down a path which led to a lonely cove. He often used it for his evening bathe and it was hidden from the main beach by a headland.

As he'd hoped he found the cove deserted and he began to swim powerfully, skirting the headland. The water was warm and without a ripple. Soon he was almost half-way over, enjoying himself in the swooning sea. He was enjoying himself till he saw the launch. A man shouted but Bentinck didn't answer. He heard the crack of a rifle and then another. The second shot came very close to his head.

Richard Bentinck put it down hard and dived.

The longshoreman had swung the tiller but Russell had acted on urgent reflex. He had grabbed it—there was an undignified scuffle. The longshoreman stood up to pull harder, Charles Russell pushed his stomach shrewdly. He went overboard with a noisy splash.

All longshoremen, Russell thought, could swim. Or wasn't that true? He'd discover later.

He turned the bows of the dinghy towards the launch, then slid the outboard motor to neutral. The launch had lost way and was barely moving. The man with the rifle had put it down but both men had glasses out and were staring.

Charles Russell stared too at the motionless sea.... He'll have to come up soon for air.

When he did so it was a yard from Russell. 'Mr Bentinck, I presume,' he said.

'That's me.' He had his head up now but the launch wasn't firing.

'I'm delighted that you've consented to meet me.' Russell spoke with a certain bland acidity; he helped Bentinck into the dinghy politely. By Charles Russell's book he wasn't first class but he seemed to be a very cool hand. 'The explanations will have to come later. For the moment it's what to do. You tell me.'

'Would you take me across?'

'With the greatest pleasure. But I don't think it's a good idea. That launch is faster than us by knots. Also they're armed and we are not.'

Richard Bentinck was watching the launch and thinking; he said finally: 'I know this country. Look, that launch isn't moving or even shouting. They could pick us off as we sit here talking but the man with the rifle has put it down. What do you make of that?'

'I don't.'

'They're radioing for further instructions. Their orders were to stop me leaving and they were ready to shoot to do just that. But they've no orders to start a general shoot-up—a longshoreman's dinghy with God knows who.'

'You're persuasive,' Charles Russell said.

'I *know*. It's a very bureaucratic country. Would you fancy a bet?'

'I bet with money but not with lives.'

'Then you drop over and swim to that launch. It's

humanly certain they weren't shooting at you. I'll take this dinghy on and chance it.'

'I think that's an even worse suggestion.' Charles Russell had quietly made his decision; he put the motor in gear and turned the dinghy. 'But I very much hope you're right,' he said.

Richard Bentinck looked back at the launch. 'She's not moving.'

'She doesn't have to move to shoot us.'

They chugged slowly across the placid sea, hailing the longshoreman, swimming strongly, not stopping to answer his outraged bawling. They beached the dinghy and Charles Russell, meticulous, pinned a five-pound note on the wooden thwart. 'I promised him four and have paid him two. The other three are for having to swim for it.'

They went to Dick Bentinck's car by the jetty. Inside Russell asked him: 'What happens now?'

'I'll take you to my temporary office.'

'You've had several bad ideas this morning and that one is the worst of all. Consider, since you must, the facts. They dislike you enough to fire shots from a rifle to say nothing of trying to burn you alive——'

'I haven't thanked you for that yet.'

'I beg you to leave it. So if you go to your office they'll pick you up.'

'I was going to go underground.'

'But where? Have you a hide-out ready?'

'No.'

'I don't know what hand you're playing yet, that's something I'll have to discuss with you later, but meanwhile my own position has changed. Up to now I've been a blameless tourist. Even that affair at your house could have seemed to them what in fact it was, an unfortunate piece of unplanned interference. But it could hardly be something quite unplanned that I happened to be around this morning. Maybe I didn't foresee a shooting but evidently I was coming to see you.' Charles Russell shook his distinguished head. 'If they pick you up they'll take me too. When neither of us is the slightest use in a matter I'm sure has importance for both of us.'

'Then what do we do?'

'You said one thing sensible. We need a hide-out and we need it at once.'

'Do you have one yourself?'

'Of course I don't. But I do have a friend who might possibly find one. To reach her I must first reach a telephone.'

'There's one in the chandler's down on the quay.'

As he climbed from the car Charles Russell asked: 'How much time do we have before they come after us?'

'With luck we ought to have twenty minutes. It depends on those men in the launch with their radio. They'll be through by now but I don't know to whom. This isn't a country where officials act quickly.'

Russell trotted to the quayside chandler where he rang to the number Gael Milo had given him. He hadn't been confident that a call to it would go through cleanly but Gael's voice was on the line at once.

'Is this line secure?'

'No line in this country is quite secure. This one is more secure than most.'

He told her what had happened briefly. 'Wait,' she said. 'I'll have to think.'

He waited for a precious minute. 'Are you there still?'

'I am. There's that hut in the mountains we still keep on. Milo keeps it for sentimental reasons and sometimes we even spend a day there. There's nobody there but a sort of *jäger*. He's reliable, he fought with Milo, but he's very poor so I'll send you food later. There's no telephone but I'm closer than you are. A good motorcyclist should get there before you. I'll arrange that he lets you in without question.'

'I'll thank you later—just now we're pressed. The map reference, please.'

'I'll get it at once.'

She was back very quickly and read it precisely. A remarkable woman, he thought, a jewel, the perfect wife for a man like Milo. It had all been as smooth as a good staff conference. 'You're kind,' he said.

'There is much between us. You'd better move fast, though. I'll contact you later.'

This time Charles Russell actually ran, something he hadn't ventured for years. In the car he said briskly: 'You've maps, I see.' He pulled one out and pointed a fingernail. 'Up there in the high hills. It's cold. You'll have to borrow the caretaker's clothes to live.' He looked at his watch: seven minutes had gone. 'If your guess at twenty minutes was right we've a start of exactly thirteen when they chase us. Someone will see which way we go, it's always like that when you want it otherwise. The north-east road out of town, then I'll guide you.'

They drove through the town and the coastal strip, climbing steadily through the mountain valleys which were the homeland of Kamich's difficult people. This country had never been tamed by Turk, and even under another empire had been too poor to be worth the expense of subduing. Dependent it had been in name but the reality had been rudely different. From here had come not soldiers but gunmen, for the people of this hard lean land had been allergic to any military discipline. They tilled their poor plots and lived austerely: the ambition of any man of this country was to see a son enter the state university. From this bitter land came the young intellectuals, not the boys from the North who were born to state service and had in fact held an old empire together, but the young with degrees and no chance of employment. They hadn't the Northerner's established connections, and the army, which would have been glad to accept them, was something which they disdained on principle as Southern and therefore alien and suspect. No wonder they often pointlessly rioted.

Charles Russell had never much cared for these people any more than he'd taken a fancy to Kamich. You couldn't deny a real respect, but their virtues were dour, they were seldom gay. To be fair to them, why should they be gay? To the north was a much more civilized people with its own way of life and good jobs to support it, what Russell still privately thought of as Europe; to the South were the solid military clans with ancient customs which were sometimes barbarous. This province was the ham in the sandwich and there wasn't much fat on the frugal meat.

They were out of the foothills now and mounting. The deciduous trees had thinned, then ended, and long lines of firs and oppressive pine marched in ordered files to the lowering sky. This was forest where no bird stirred or sang. Sometimes there were sudden glimpses of the high bare mountains beyond the treeline, and once there was a sight of snow. Russell was reading the contour lines carefully and he knew they weren't going as high as that. Just the same it was getting uncomfortably cold. Russell had given his jacket to Bentinck. Both men were shivering, Bentinck the more, but Charles Russell was not surprised at that. He kept his London maisonette at something round sixty-five degrees, but Bentinck was an American who would keep wherever he lived nearly seventy and at the least excuse would raise that steeply. Russell was chilled in his summer shirt-sleeves but he hadn't yet began to suffer. Bentinck had clenched his teeth to stop their noise.

They had climbed perhaps four thousand feet, the road swinging round the mountain's shoulder. Mostly the curves were much too sharp to see more than a hundred yards behind them but here there was a stretch they could see. It was probably six hundred feet lower; it was certainly six miles behind them. Bentinck said through shut teeth:

'There's a car. It's chasing us.'

'How do you know?'

'I know the make. It's Italian and very fast, and only a certain police can have it.' He had stopped his own car and took out field-glasses. 'Yes,' he said, 'an Italian job. And they're pushing it very hard indeed.' He turned to Russell. 'How far to go?'

Russell looked at the map. 'About twenty miles.'

'Not enough,' Bentinck said.

'But they must be at least six miles behind us. Once we've reached where we're going and got inside I would very much doubt if they'll come in after us. They'll know to whom this cabin belongs, and you said yourself that this isn't a country where officials like to make quick decisions. They'll do what those men in the launch did too, they'll radio for further instructions. And I don't think there's yet a man in this country who'd make an arrest on Milo's property without reference to Milo himself. All that is going to take time—perhaps days.'

'You may well be right. If we ever get there.'

'We're wasting time talking. Let's give them a run.'

Richard Bentinck shook his head regretfully. 'They'll catch us well short of that hut. They've the legs on us.'

On reflection Charles Russell was inclined to agree. The American consul's American car was a desirable piece of engineering on wide flat roads with gentle curves but in the mountains it was a lumbering cow. You had to haul it round corners on squealing tyres, the brakes had begun to fade already, and if you drove it fast in the lower gears the engine would at best be suspect. A modern high-revving Italian car would catch them well within twenty miles even giving them a six-mile start.

Richard Bentinck said uncertainly: 'Walk?'

'Leave the road and walk through the mountains? Not on.' Charles Russell was speaking from hard experience. 'If it's twenty by road then it's forty off it, and even assuming I picked the best route, something I couldn't guarantee, that's the best part of two days' very hard walking. Light Infantry pace at that,' he added. 'With proper clothes I'd take it on, but a night in the mountains in what we stand in and I don't think we'd move very far next day.'

'Then there's only one thing for it.'

'Tell me.'

Bentinck pointed at a fallen fir. 'Could we shift that together?'

'I dare say we could. Also I don't see the slightest point. You must forgive me if I risk a quotation. An obstacle uncovered by fire is no obstacle.'

'I wasn't thinking of trying to shoot it out.'

'No?' Russell said. 'Then what were you thinking?'

'I was thinking that we've stopped on a corner. It is also a very blind corner indeed.' Bentinck pointed across the road at the unfenced side. 'Six hundred feet drop and maybe more. Of course we'd leave that tree trunk slant-ing. A secret policeman comes round driving hard ...' He shrugged.

'You're a pretty hard man,' Charles Russell said. But he had climbed out of the car to say it.

'I've got a job to do. I get paid to do it.' They had begun to haul on the fallen fir. 'Also, remember, they tried to burn me. Alive, as it happened. I didn't like that.'

'You talk almost like an Englishman.'

'Do I?' They had moved the fir, not a big one but adequate: their own car they had left beyond it. 'For good measure they shot at an unarmed swimmer. You spoke of arrest—they're more likely to shoot again.'

'I've helped you move that tree,' Russell said. 'I don't think you'd have done it alone.' For necessity he had no regrets.

Richard Bentinck said without emotion: 'Life in this country is very cheap. I'm afraid that would go for us too. No, I know it.'

Russell nodded as they went back to the car. He had earlier and impressive experience that the statement was alarmingly true.

8

Richard Bentinck and Russell had finished their breakfast
—black bread and sour cream but the coffee was excellent.
The *jäger* hadn't commented that two total strangers, one
more than half naked, had descended on him in the name
of his premier, indeed he hadn't a language to comment
in since Bentinck couldn't speak his own nor he the
normal lingua franca. But he had clothed them as best he
could. Bentinck was wearing moleskin trousers and a shirt
which though ancient was spotlessly clean and a sort of
poshteen which would keep out the cold. Charles Russell
who'd at least had a suit had been provided with a very
thick jersey.

After breakfast they moved to the fire and waited. The
jäger seemed in no hurry whatever. Russell had noticed
that over the fireplace hung a modern rifle beautifully
kept. Bentinck tried him again in the lingua franca but
the *jäger* shook his head in apology. He was old and lined
but wiry and active, essentially the mountain recluse.
Richard Bentinck said, a little uneasily:

'What we ate this morning was two days' rations.'

'My friends promised food.'

'I hope that they're quick with it. We can't eat him
out of house and home.'

As if reading the thought the *jäger* rose. He took down
the rifle and loaded it carefully; he made a gesture which

said as clearly as words: 'I'm going out hunting so wish me good fortune.' He left and they watched him walk up to the tree line. He walked slowly but with the stride of the mountains. It was long and deliberate, he could hold it all day.

When the *jäger* had gone Bentinck turned to Russell. They had spoken together the night before, briefly but enough to make clear they were men with a common and urgent problem. The word 'alliance' had never been used but both men knew that it now existed. Necessity needed no formal contract.

'What I don't understand,' Charles Russell said, 'is how an expert like Shaw came to miss that gold.'

'I think that puts it a little severely. He didn't exactly miss it; he didn't look. His job was to assess iron ore—how much and how rich and how easy to work. He did that very thoroughly but when he came to the end of the lode he stopped. He didn't go looking for something else which in fact was several miles from the iron. Not that that would matter much once your company had put down the railroad.'

'Then how was it found?'

'In a sense by accident. Milo's a properly cautious man, and since Shaw was checking on Milo's iron he sent up a team to check on Shaw. That was sensible, I'd have done it myself. I'd have wanted to be sure what was covered before signing any form of contract. So this team goes much wider than Shaw's ever needed to. What they stumbled on wasn't only gold; they stumbled on political dynamite.'

'Internationally?'

'To my country especially. The almighty dollar is very sick.'

Charles Russell was silent, thinking it over, but he was also considering Richard Bentinck. He had thought him at one time half-way to a strongarm, people whom Russell would use but disliked, but he was a man who would face his own mistakes and now he rather admired Richard Bentinck. But no, he thought quickly, that wasn't precise: what he really felt was respect, even envy. To Richard Bentinck the United States was the country to which he owed allegiance. It was perfectly natural to serve it blindly, sometimes dangerously but never tortured by doubt. He lifted Charles Russell's own doubting heart. Sometimes it had seemed to him, reading his daily paper unhappily, that the irony column, designed to amuse him, was the only piece of sane reporting, perhaps the only piece of straight reporting. A soldier couldn't shoot a terrorist without a judge being sent on the farce of inquiry. Russell had almost lost the habit of thinking in terms of countries or nations. All he'd been able to do in his service was put an elbow in the leaking dams. Beyond them were the threatening waters, muddied by flaccid thinking and envy. Perhaps the dams would hold for his lifetime, in which case he wouldn't see the flood. He didn't hope for much more for he didn't dare to. Being Head of the Security Executive had taught him who were his world's real enemies. Many were very far from communism.

He said thoughtfully: 'How do *you* know this?'

'Because it was leaked. One of the team which Milo sent up there had loyalties in another country. He leaked it to them, where we've lines of our own. When the story came through to the men who employ me they went straight to the top. Where of course the top panicked.'

'And why do that?'

Richard Bentinck's eyes opened wide in surprise. It occurred to him he was having his leg pulled but Charles Russell's voice had held no irony. Bentinck's final decision was near the truth. This urbane and remarkably well-preserved Englishman was ignorant of all economics. He'd been warned that this could sometimes happen, particularly with men of this type, and that when it did it was very misleading. These men were in no way less shrewd and ruthless that they were indifferent to what you'd been taught at Harvard. Richard Bentinck began to explain the essentials.

Charles Russell had none of his chairman's mistrust for men who might carry the label economist and he listened with an increasing interest.... It was much too easy and much too slick to talk contemptuously of digging up gold, then burying it in another country, in a Fort where it earned no interest whatever. Whether you liked the system or not, and those who disliked it most were the eggheads, gold was still the main backing of major currencies, which in practice meant international trade. Of course it might be demonetized sometime, though not, Bentinck thought, in anyone's lifetime. In which case it would follow silver and look how the Silver States had squawked. Gold stocks as they stood in the world today would meet industrial demand for at least a century.

Charles Russell had listened, bemused but fascinated. This was the background, the bite was coming.

So Bretton Woods had broken down and nobody quite knew what was coming. The dollar was in effect inconvertible and an official price of thirty-eight dollars a very poor jest in the open market. Then what did you do, did you face reality, letting gold run to its proper price? There were sensible people who thought that sensible but the politics were all against them. Nine men out of ten, including Frenchmen, who talked glibly of something they called the gold standard were in fact using words with imprecision. What they meant was the gold *exchange* standard—different. An alternative was bits of paper, as a matter of academics a starter, but you needed more trust than at present existed to hand your standard of life to some faceless body known only by a clutch of initials. So more gold in the world would be no bad thing, it might even solve pressing intractable problems. There was a proviso though, and a very big one. It would have to be used within the rules, not primarily as a political weapon. Used as that, as in certain hands it would be, it could be every bit as destructive and final as some invention for changing a continent's climate.

Charles Russell had nodded; he felt firm ground. He hadn't been trained in these arcane mysteries but he could recognize a political danger and he knew from a lifetime of grim experience how a country under pressure reacted. He inquired at once:

'So what were your orders?'

'A watching brief—for the moment no more. But what my masters dare not and will not accept is control of that gold from east of here. I've told you why and I don't exaggerate. My orders were to watch developments, to report any sign of Milo weakening.'

'Weakening from what?' Russell asked.

'From his intention to sign a contract with Commonwealth. Commonwealth is okay with us.'

'You knew about that?'

'Oh yes, we knew that. We also knew that when in London Milo had called on a Colonel Charles Russell. Who is currently a director of Commonwealth but who also has—may I say?—a record.' Bentinck added with a touch of naiveté: 'That's why when you called the other day I didn't want to be seen to be talking publicly.'

Charles Russell reflected, his face expressionless. He liked this young man and privately envied him. He might not be exceptionally clever but he had something more important than cleverness. Richard Bentinck had a simple fidelity. Charles Russell decided to move a step further.

'Did you know that Milo had fallen sick?'

'We know he's had a couple of strokes.'

'Did you know he'd just had a third?'

'We did not.' Richard Bentinck sat up. 'That's extremely awkward.'

'Who do you think is going to succeed him?'

'Anything could happen here, it's far from what it appears on the surface. But the form horse is undoubtedly Kamich.' Bentinck was uneasy and showing it. 'Kamich would honour Milo's contract, then he'd find some excuse to sequester the lot. After that he would lean the wrong way; he'd be forced to. Milo has prestige and charisma, he could stand up to pressure and probably would. But Kamich is just a party boss from the least of three races which hates the others. I don't think he'd stand when the heat came on him, and that heat would come on very quickly indeed.'

Charles Russell considered this in turn. It wasn't so far from his own opinion, reinforced by a knowledge he couldn't share since it had come to him as a director of Commonwealth, the knowledge of an unexplained shareholding.... 'Commonwealth is okay with us,' but 'okay' was hardly a term of art. Was Commonwealth okay with them? It was probably okay with Bentinck but the Bentincks didn't make higher policy. Bentinck would see a

British concern which whatever else it was or wasn't was presumably on the same side of the line, but his masters would look beyond the company to a country which couldn't defend its interests. Russell had listened to Bentinck carefully, and though he hadn't been able to follow the details an experienced nose had smelt a crisis. This matter of gold was much too serious to be left in the hands of a second-class Power. Bentinck's masters would never consent to do so, indeed all the signals were flashing strongly that they'd started to cut themselves in already. ... Mid Western, Charles Russell remembered—a giant. A giant with a colossus behind it, a colossus if not with feet of clay then apparently with feet of gold. Mid Western had twenty per cent already, or if it hadn't that holding made little sense. Twenty per cent was well short of control but you didn't need fifty-one per cent to have effective control in decisions which mattered. Thirty per cent, Russell guessed, would give that.

He said nothing of this to Bentinck; he dare not. He had assessed Richard Bentinck from much knowledge of men. He was a man you could take to shoot a tiger but he hadn't the weight and far less the experience to be safe in a major operation. If it came to that in this very strange country, so smooth in its civilized western veneer, below it old customs quite often savage, they'd use somebody of much heavier metal. But Bentinck didn't seem to realize it. He was saying on a note of resentment:

'We're useless here—in hiding, helpless. There isn't even a telephone.'

'No. But assuming there were a telephone, assuming you could get a call through, assuming the line wasn't tapped six times over—assuming all that may I ask what you'd say?'

'I'd like to report that Milo's ill again. Also the fact we've been chased up here. That means that something bad is brewing.'

'You're right,' Russell said but he didn't say more. Richard Bentinck was a loyal servant and the organization which quietly employed him was one which Charles Russell had always respected. Its failures were more unkindly publicized than the successes it seldom claimed for the record, and Charles Russell thanked his God it existed. But it wasn't its country's sole source of power, which had levers in this one and would probably pull them. It armed the army, the air force too; it gave public aid and a secret subsidy.

Russell looked at Dick Bentinck but didn't utter. The next move would certainly come from America but not from the people whom Bentinck worked for.

Charles Russell's guess had also been right: the next move by Richard Bentinck's country was not to send new orders to Bentinck, far less to replace him with heavier metal, but to send in its ambassador with instructions to lean on these people discreetly. He'd already been told what he had to protect, an interest which the dispatch had described as even more important than oil, but he didn't intend to do any leaning. He had been in Milo's country some time and he reckoned that he knew the people. They reacted very strongly indeed to anything suggesting bullying. So instead of throwing his weight about he had decided to offer reassurance.

Moreover events had improved his hand. Ambassadors called on Foreign Ministers and that Minister was a man called Kamich whose private policies and suspected leanings were precisely what was causing alarm. He'd get nowhere by a call on Kamich, but to try to contact Milo direct would be irregular besides being dangerous. Apart from the breach of protocol, which this ambassador was too wise to be slave to, such a visit would be known in minutes. It would promptly alert the other side and so make future action more difficult. But Milo, as it had broken, was sick. It would be quite in order, perfectly natural, to call on his wife with flowers and a message. She might not know the actual details of what his dispatch had somewhat coyly referred to as even more important than oil but she was known to have her husband's ear and for the moment that was more than enough.

Gael received him with a quiet composure though the call was in fact an inconvenience. She had been considering another matter, Charles Russell and the American consul holed up in a hut where they wouldn't now be unless she had asked Charles Russell to help her; she couldn't escape her responsibility even if she had wished to do so; she had promised them food and meant to send it that morning, and they'd need more than mere food. They would need protection.

When the ambassador rang she'd been making her plans but when his call came through she put them off, accepting his splendid roses gracefully. He was a man she had always liked and got on with for he had none of the airs and foolish graces which in European diplomats were something which raised her hackles resentfully. He was a professional and he knew his job. He was also an easy man to talk to. He said at once:

'This is very sad news.'

'My husband is a little better.'

'I'm delighted to hear it.' He sounded delighted.

She was perfectly content to wait. She knew all about this ambassador's background. He came from the squarest of all Square States and was properly proud he was no sort of egghead. As far as this excellent man was concerned the eastern coast, California too, could float away into their respective oceans and he wouldn't lose a minute of sleep. He was a man who would play his hand with skill but he didn't suppose there was any mystique in it. When he saw she was waiting for him to lead he said in his simple friendly manner:

'We knew he'd had two attacks before.'

She decided there was no point in concealment, he had means to discover the truth if she tried. 'The doctors tell me he isn't likely to die but he'll never be the man he was.'

'Then I've come here to offer my country's assurances in a matter which I believe you will guess.'

'May I take it you mean who is going to succeed him if Milo should decide to retire?'

The ambassador nodded. 'You may indeed. So you can see that we have an interest in common.'

'In common,' she said, 'but not quite the same. But I agree that a common problem exists.'

'Exactly why I have ventured to call on you. I repeat my country's firmest assurances.' For the first and last time he was almost formal.

She knew exactly what the ambassador meant. If Milo's policy survived his retirement then the American horn of plenty stayed open, the tanks for the army at knockdown prices, the open aid and the secret subsidy. If policy changed ...

She didn't know. It was unlikely they'd face intervention directly and certainly not another Vietnam but they could make life very hard indeed. She wouldn't blame them for that since one didn't aid enemies. Only the

British fell for that in odd corners of what had once been an empire which now secretly hated and would never support them. She decided to put out another feeler.

'If Milo retires—when Milo retires—there's bound to be an internal power struggle.'

'I'm afraid there is,' the ambassador said.

'Which way do you think it's going to go?'

His Excellency didn't answer at once. He was uncertain how far it was wise to go, but she had offered a fly. He decided to take it.

'There's one person who could guarantee that your husband's sane policy still continues.'

She read his meaning and didn't attempt to duck. There wasn't any advantage in ducking. 'I'm out of touch,' she said.

'The South would be behind you solidly, and the South, as you very well know, means the army.'

'I don't want a civil war.'

'Nor do we. But we'd prefer it to a puppet government.'

'You're very frank.'

'I have found it pays. We don't want another satellite state and there's a man in the running who would take you that way.'

'If you're thinking of whom I believe you are I think you do him some injustice. Whatever he is he's not a traitor.'

'I agree with you—I think that too. But we don't believe he could ride the wind, not with his record and private sympathies. Perhaps our enemies wouldn't risk an invasion, but the pressures would go on increasingly and I don't think he'd have the support to resist them.'

'You may well be right.'

'Or I may be wrong. Ambassadors don't make a country's

policy and haven't for a very long time. What they do is carry out their instructions and mine are to offer you every support. That's a general statement but also particular.' He rose and held out his hand. 'I mean that personally. May I hope that you'll at least consider it.'

·'I'll consider because I must,' she said.

When he'd gone she went back to her desk and her planning.... Charles Russell and that American consul. The ambassador hadn't mentioned him though he must know that he wasn't attending his office. He must also know Bentinck's work outside it, but this matter had now moved much higher up than some plot by Richard Bentinck's employers. Whatever she had to face in the future it wouldn't be that sort of secret warfare.

She began to give clear and succinct orders. An estate car was to be loaded with food and driven to the hut with a guard. Gael had decided who that should be. She was specializing in tourists now but once she'd been Gael's personal bodyguard. Gael had liked Magda as guard and person, a woman of her own tough people and one she could trust to keep her mouth shut. She was bold and resourceful, she got on with men. Gael Milo smiled a woman's smile. Magda certainly did that, she remembered. It was a pity she couldn't speak much English but Magda would make herself understood. She managed that very well indeed.

Gael went to her husband's room to tell him, not of Russell and Bentinck chased up to the mountains, an impertinence which would mean one of his tantrums, but of the fact of the ambassador's call. She found him sitting propped up by pillows and she took his hand and awaited his pleasure. His skin was the colour of drying putty and his deep strong voice had notably weakened. He said in it before she could speak:

'I have something to tell you. Perhaps I should have told you before—normally we share all secrets. But you had worries enough. A fresh attempt on my life ...'

His voice tailed away and she thought he was sleeping but he was gathering his diminished strength. He said with something quite close to his normal vigour:

'Up in those mountains—there's gold there too. It could drag us into the twentieth century and there's one place it must never go.'

She started to speak but stopped at once. This time he had slipped into sleep. He may die, she thought, or linger on. Either I can bear since I must but one thing I cannot bear and will not. I can't stand aside with folded hands watching the work of a lifetime crumble.

She left him to sleep and walked down to her office. As a member of the People's House she was entitled to one though she ran it modestly. She picked up a phone, then put it down. She knew now what she might have to do; she didn't yet see the way to do it.

The two men in the Alfa had so far been silent, one driving fast, the other watching. Richard Bentinck had called them secret policemen but the term would have given them much offence. They thought of themselves as aristocrats, as guardians of the public order. The watcher said:

'I can see them above us.'

'What sort of car?'

'An American monster.'

'How far ahead?'

'I'd say six miles.'

'So it's twenty for them, twenty-six for us. We can catch them, all right.'

He began to do so. His fast driving was now very close to brilliance but it was his speed which gave him no chance whatever against the fir tree on a very blind corner. He had a split second to use his brakes and did so but a split second was very much less than enough. The watcher had time to open and jump but his momentum rolled him helplessly forward. Forward and over. He went with a scream.

The driver's face was a mask of fear. The car hit the tree trunk; it slithered sideways. For a moment it teetered, then it went too.

It fell cleanly, all six hundred feet. When it hit it began to burn at once.

9

The man who had come to call on Lord Tokenhouse had been a Minister, not a hack from the Foreign Office, and he'd put it as a request for help in the simple language which Tokenhouse liked. There'd been a telegram from an ambassador, the one in Milo's most difficult country. It had been full of diplomatic flannel but when you'd boiled out the fat the message was simple. Charles Russell who now sat on Commonwealth's board but had once been something strikingly different had gone down to Milo's country on holiday. Perhaps the caller might say on ostensible holiday without Lord Tokenhouse thinking him merely impertinent. There something had happened or maybe it hadn't—that part of the message was far from clear, a typical piece of F.O. blather. What was known was that this director of Commonwealth had an international reputation in a field which was very different from mining. It might all be absurdly suspicious and silly but in a country like that it was quite understandable. They now wanted him out of their hair and quickly and had said so through their Foreign Minister. Naturally it would all be smoother if they weren't obliged to take formal action, and Lord Tokenhouse, as the chairman of Commonwealth, could let them off what they saw as a hook. Very likely there was no hook at all, but Milo's country was an important one, important between East and West, and the Minister would be greatly obliged if Lord Tokenhouse saw the matter with sympathy. The Minister had picked up his hat. He'd been good at his job and had said all he needed.

Lord Tokenhouse had shown him out. Charles Russell, he decided quickly, had quite properly gone to Milo's country on the holiday he had said he was taking, maybe also to visit old friends and scenes. There he had stumbled on something—that gold. Lord Tokenhouse had had Milo's authority to tell his board when the time was ripe but he hadn't yet exercised his option and he wouldn't until another matter was clearer. He was thinking of the new holding in Commonwealth, twenty per cent and a nuisance potentially, but within ten or so of effective control. He'd been convinced that the holders were really Mid Western but much less convinced of Mid Western's motive. It couldn't be iron, they had more than enough of it, but if they'd even the faintest smell of that gold there'd be much more than merely commercial motives, there'd be enormous political pressures behind them. Meanwhile he must tell his board about Russell. He'd have been happy to have decided alone but it was foolish to expose yourself when cover was there for the simple asking.

So now he was looking round Commonwealth's table. Commonwealth had a longstanding tradition that its board should be kept as small as possible and Lord Tokenhouse supported it strongly. Just Weston, the man of many boards, Macrae the accountant and Shaw the expert. With Russell that made a comfortable five but with Russell away they were only four. If they broke two-two Lord Tokenhouse thought, he'd be obliged to use a casting vote and he was sufficiently an orthodox chairman to detest the idea of exposing his neck. He could be arbitrary but not for the record.

He told them about his visitor shortly. 'Your friend was pretty cool,' Weston said.

'I've already sent a telegram asking for Russell's return at once.'

'Then why are we meeting?'

'You misunderstand me. I sent it before the Minister called. I wanted Russell for consultation. Political consultation. Very.'

'Then you think that this cock and bull F.O. story——'

'I cannot be said to be properly thinking since I haven't the real facts before me. I've told you what I know, which is little. If you like to oversimplify you could say that a Minister is asking a favour.'

'I can think of one reason not to grant it.' It was Macrae, the accountant, solid and practical.

'Then tell us, please.'

'It's a negative reason. You said that you'd called him back already. May we know what he answered?'

'He hasn't answered.'

'Not even excuses?'

'Nothing at all.'

'Then suppose we send him a board's instruction and suppose he doesn't comply with that.' Macrae was a Scot with a Scot's sense of discipline. Disobedience to a formal order would be something to offend him deeply. It followed he would do much to avoid it. He was doing it now. 'We should walk very carefully.'

'You're thinking of the sanctions available?'

'You could put it like that.'

'I do put it like that.'

Shaw said brutally: 'You could simply sack him.' He had always resented Charles Russell's presence, an outsider who knew nothing of mining.

Lord Tokenhouse pounced on this at once. 'Mr Shaw, I am sorry to have to say it, but the suggestion is both out of order and foolish. As chairman of this company I can decide what duties directors carry, but all directors have been put on this board by the shareholders in open meeting and I can no more dismiss one than you sack me.'

'Suspend him then,' Shaw said. He was stubborn.

But Macrae shook his head at once and decisively. For one thing he admired Charles Russell, who had the graces which he knew he hadn't, and for another he liked things done in form. 'Suspend him from what?' he asked. 'He does nothing. He hasn't any executive duties.'

'The point is well taken,' Lord Tokenhouse said.

'But not quite completely.' It was Weston again. He had scented which way the meeting was going and as usual intended to lean the right way. 'We can certainly order him back—why not? But any talk of enforcement is futile in practice. Russell isn't a City guinea-pig; he has a pension and I believe some money. He may simply put his holiday first, especially as he went on it with the chairman's knowledge and full consent. Charles Russell could leave this board tomorrow and the leaving, to him, would be no disaster.'

'It might be to us,' Macrae said grimly. 'The legal aspect deserves some thought. Suppose he's gone off on some tourists' coach trip—he could hardly have left an address for forwarding; or suppose he's simply fallen ill. So we suspend him unilaterally without giving him a chance to be heard and we'll have a writ round our necks which will cost us our shirts.'

'Charles Russell would never do that.'

'I know. The point is that Charles Russell could.' James

Macrae was now very dour indeed. 'I would like that on the record, please.'

Lord Tokenhouse looked round again. They had had their say as most men must, they were ready to accept a lead. 'So the question is of means not ends. We should summon him back and I use the word carefully. The question is of the summons' form.'

'An appeal to his better nature,' Shaw said. As irony it fell dead, stillborn.

The chairman said blandly: 'That's excellent. The wording ...?' Nobody answered him. 'Then I'll have to make it up myself. I'll remind him of my previous telegram which after all was a purely personal message, then I'll continue that since the date I sent it we've all of us had the chance to discuss and we're all of us now of a single mind. Charles Russell is the man we need. A little modest flattery is acceptable even to men like Russell. As for the hypothetical question, what we do if he doesn't choose to return, I suggest that we should deal with it as hypothetical questions are mostly best dealt with. I suggest that we leave it until it arises.' He looked round for the final time. 'Dissent?'

Nobody spoke and the chairman rose.

When the others had gone Lord Tokenhouse smiled. He was a very experienced chairman indeed with all the arts of his trade at sensitive fingertips and it had given him a real satisfaction to have handled his meeting as well as he had. So he smiled but he was also worried, though not because of the Board of Commonwealth and certainly not for its absent member. What was worrying him was a paragraph which he'd noticed in the midday paper. It had been tucked away on a middle page with political news not considered worth comment but to Lord Tokenhouse it was a flaring headline. A man called Milo had fallen ill. How ill he was was not yet known since the bulletins were being cagey but he'd cancelled several public engagements.

Lord Tokenhouse remembered Sir Jonathan Something. The idiot had been talking of iron, suggesting it would be no bad thing if Commonwealth took in Mid Western as partners and by implication the major Power which would certainly back Mid Western in trouble. Talk about iron was by now without point, whereas talk about the need for support had been well founded and for Sir Jonathan sensible. It had been sensible but at that time not urgent. Now it was very urgent indeed. Milo wasn't young any more, and even if he wasn't dying you couldn't run a country like Milo's powder keg while you lay on a bed and fought for your health. If he died or were even obliged to retire the succession would be wide wide open. If that went the wrong way, which in practice meant Left, then Commonwealth might be out on its ear and the gold in quite other and ruthless hands which would use it for international mischief. Lord Tokenhouse was no economist but knew more than enough to realize the danger. Somehow they'd have to contrive to block it but any action would have to be his alone.

He sighed for he wanted to talk to Russell. Russell, like himself, thought politically, something the rest of his board did not. It had been one of his reasons for not yet telling them; he'd tell them when it was cut and dried, when their astonishment and conceivably protest would be powerless to affect events. One thing was perfectly clear to Lord Tokenhouse. He had a public duty and meant to do it.

He sighed again at 'public duty' for there were people who wouldn't consider it that, they'd consider it a social crime. Fighting to keep a material asset—the action was wicked as a matter of principle. Gold belonged to the world, to the U.N.O., to Indira Gandhi, to the angels in heaven. For the rich to protect their wealth was sin, and the fact that the alternative was financial chaos and maybe collapse was something of no account whatever. The establishments, Tokenhouse thought—there were two of them. There was the hard one in the City and industry where profit was still a respectable word and the soft where it was earnestly suspect, the consensus-minded politicians in their clubs where the food was bad, the wine worse, the critics with little beards and paunches, the ladies who lived in north-west London on social consciences and private means, the whole *lumpenintelligentsia*. Lord Tokenhouse much preferred a good communist. At least they had shown they could run an empire.

But he didn't intend to let them have it, not this gold which they'd use to bring down his world. There'd be a price and he was prepared to pay it. That price was effective control of his company.

It cut deeply against the grain to concede it. His Afrikaner grandfather had founded the firm in some dusty dorp, and then, as it expanded and flourished, his father had moved its headquarters to London. By now it was English in name and habit and its major interests were international. But Tokenhouse still had South African kinsmen who'd inherited shares and kept them from sentiment. They wouldn't much like what he meant to do.

He rose and paced his boardroom deliberately. Mid Western had twenty per cent already, or if it hadn't he was a monkey's uncle: another ten in their hands would settle it finally—Mid Western and the great Power behind them. Lord Tokenhouse still held more than ten but he couldn't sell direct to Mid Western. To do so without telling his board would be grossly improper and maybe more, and if he told them there'd have to be explanations at a moment when what he wished least in the world was explaining the facts to astonished men who'd ask all the right questions but not think politically.

Auntie Mabel—she was near to death. Auntie Mabel had twelve per cent of Commonwealth. She also had landed property but it was entailed on a very much younger nephew. There'd be danegeld to pay in the form of Duty and the family wanted to keep the land. The obvious course was to sell the shares, the less obvious was to sell them wisely. Wisely now meant as Lord Tokenhouse wished.

He went back to his office and rang New York. He had a contact there whom he trusted fully. He explained and the line went suddenly silent.

'Are you there still?'

'I am. And I've understood you. I will see that your message reaches its target. Naturally your name won't be mentioned.'

Lord Tokenhouse put the receiver down happily. That was pretty close to the wind, he thought, but it's much better than the cold blast from the steppes.

For once Bojalian wasn't bullying and Kamich was more than ever on guard. Greeks bearing gifts were proverbially dangerous, and Armenians being conciliatory were either in a hopeless position or else believed that they had you cold. Kamich in this case suspected the latter and he listened with an increasing suspicion. Bojalian was saying importantly but with notably less than his usual venom:

'I could let you off two hooks, you know—a big one and another smaller.'

'Let's have the big one first.'

'As you please. I've been in touch with the very highest circles.' Bojalian's manner was now plain pompous. 'I can offer a very fair proposition, indeed I think it's extremely generous. I will put it in the simplest terms. You will keep your gold and all that it means to you. We shall make no attempt to interfere. In return you will sell it to us—every ounce of it.'

'Who finances its working?'

'We will do that.'

'And you say that you'll never interfere?'

'If you keep your side of the bargain why should we?'

Kamich could think of a dozen reasons but he had a question still and that question was vital. 'So we hand you whatever we manage to mine. May I ask at what price?'

'At a fixed price, naturally.'

'What is that price?'

'That's a matter for detailed negotiation.'

Kamich was silent; he thought it typical. In one sense the offer was not ungenerous, assuming they would keep their word, which was a very big assumption indeed. But in another it ran to form depressingly. They simply couldn't resist temptation, to set a snare, somehow to best you. Byzantium was too deep in their blood to allow of anything straight and watertight. The opportunity to twist must be there. If Kamich agreed with the price still open his guess was that they'd offer the worst one, the thirty-eight dollars now doubtfully formal. But in the open market gold was climbing, already well over seventy dollars and with signals set for a further rise. Kamich didn't yet know how deep he could go in an open market the world's bankers detested, but with Commonwealth holding the main concession he suspected it wouldn't be very far. They would make some arrangement to suit the West since they'd have more than a feeble Whitehall behind them.

'You'll realize I can't decide in a minute.'

To his surprise Bojalian nodded agreement. 'I realize that but there isn't much time. Events are moving against us strongly.'

'You mean Milo's illness? That's public now.'

'Milo's illness and also the matter of Russell. Charles Russell and that American Bentinck.' Bojalian looked at Kamich coolly. 'I know where they're hiding,' he said. 'I traced them.'

Kamich would have given much to explode in an immediate temper but he controlled himself with an evident effort. That would serve no purpose, or none at the moment. It was an impertinence that this cocky Armenian was running something approaching a regular network and openly telling Kamich he did so, but its extent and its power were still unknown. So far it had done nothing remarkable, and it was an axiom of all counter-intelligence not to act before you had all the facts. These agents, if that were the proper word, had followed Russell to Richard Bentinck's house, hardly a feat which a competent man would claim as an outstanding triumph, then they'd traced both men to Milo's cabin. That again had been something quite close to routine. A police car had left the town in a hurry, taking a road which was little used and which ended in a mountain village. You had only to follow that road on a map, you had only to know what many did, that Milo had a hut in the mountains, and your guess could be confirmed by inspection.

'I hope your men made the journey safely.' He had

spoken with sarcasm which was promptly returned.

'As I gather that your first lot did not. Yes, thank you, they weren't in a tearing hurry. By the time your second car came up, looking for the first, I imagine, they had seen what they wanted and quietly gone home.'

'That second car found the first one wrecked. They also found two policemen, dead.'

'Whom no doubt you will wish to avenge.'

'In good time.'

Surprisingly Bojalian made no protest. 'I'm a reasonable man,' he said, and for once he sounded almost that. 'I can see that you're in a very real difficulty. Those two in that hut are in Milo's protection and to take action while he is still alive, fading perhaps but still holding the reins, would be premature and maybe dangerous.' Something of his bullying manner returned. 'Quite possibly dangerous to you yourself. Milo has never fancied liberties and that would be a very large one.'

Kamich didn't answer this since the statement had been entirely correct. When the moment came to challenge Milo he wouldn't shrink from the extremes of violence, but nor would he risk a major target for the pleasure of avenging two policemen. He said in his smoothest, most worldly voice, the manner he'd used when he called on Russell:

'You still think Russell and Bentinck dangerous?'

'I certainly do. Consider the facts. Russell is a director of Commonwealth and Bentinck is an American agent. We both of us know what stands behind him and neither of us can take that lightly.'

'I don't see what they can do from that cabin. All they've achieved by taking refuge is to neutralize themselves effectively.'

'They wouldn't be in that cabin at all unless Milo had had some use for them. He can collect them at any moment it suits him.'

'I can't deny that on the facts we know.'

'Nor deny that these men are *potentially* dangerous?'

Kamich shook his head reluctantly.

Bojalian lit one of his dreadful smokes. 'I spoke of letting you off two hooks—we've had one. You'll need time to consider that—I concede it. The other hook is Russell and Bentinck and there I can give you no time at all.'

'That isn't letting me off a hook.'

'But it is. I can understand and I don't dissent from your reason for not taking action yourself, but some action is very urgently needed.' Bojalian was back to his earlier form. 'If you can't take it,' he said, 'I will.'

'You?' Kamich was astonished, not hiding it.

'You must forgive me if I've been reading your thoughts.' The old malice was returning strongly. 'You were thinking that to have agents here is an impertinence which you'd like to slap down. I will give you a piece of quite free information. I have agents here but they're not very good ones. They can follow people and later report; they can tap their phones, sometimes bug their houses; but I don't have a really reliable killer.'

'You'll import one then?'

'I'll do no such thing.'

'Then what will you do?'

'I shall act as I must.' Bojalian rose through the stinking smoke. 'I shall keep you in touch,' he said. 'You'll reciprocate.' It wasn't a question but an undisguised order.

When Bojalian had gone at last Kamich had time to think deliberately. He had forgotten his private debt to Charles Russell. For one thing the stakes had climbed too high, and if it came to a private justification it was one thing to order arrest or death, quite another to feel obliged to prevent it. Which in any case he dare not do. If he tried to prevent this wild plan of Bojalian's, Bojalian wouldn't be talking concessions, he'd return with a naked ultimatum.

But was it so wild? Kamich seriously wondered. There were two men in a hut and perhaps they were guarded, but this needn't be a scene from a western, the hero walking in and shooting it out. There were other weapons more deadly than pistols and Bojalian could obtain one easily. Nor was the private motive so strange when you looked at it through the eye of experience. Kamich had at first been astonished but now, on reflection, surprise diminished. He thought again of the comfortable saw, comfortable because reassuring, that bullies were always at bottom cowards. Bojalian was no sort of coward whatever but Bojalian was the classical desk man. They sat in their rooms and plotted and planned and often they did it extremely well, but in their hearts they were men who'd been unfulfilled. Desk operators—they were all the same. All of them had this itch for action, a passion for involvement in violence. Intellectuals had it too but differently. With them it was a sort of mystique and seldom if ever went further than daydreams, but the planners at desks were much more dangerous since they had the knowledge of violence staining their papers and the means to obtain what it needed in practice.

Kamich only hoped Bojalian would do his killing in a decent manner. The trouble with all amateurs was that they mostly left a disgusting mess.

10

The *jäger* returned with what looked like a goat, disembowelling it in the cabin's lean-to. Charles Russell, who had served in India, could stand horrible smells with a notable tolerance, but he wasn't surprised that Richard Bentinck, a man from a country which prized deodorants, looked queasy and then suppressed a retch. The *jäger* cooked on an open fire in the cabin's single living-room and the stew he made in an ancient black pot was a very unpleasant stew indeed. He was clearly a man who lived on little but he was still accepting the situation. Dick Bentinck couldn't speak his language but 'Milo', he had at once understood. These strangers were Milo's men. So be it. The obligations of friendship were always mandatory.

From politeness they'd started to eat his meal when the noise of a car disturbed all three of them. They all stood up and the *jäger* frowned. He took the rifle down again but Russell said 'Wait' and walked to the window. 'Not a police car or a very unusual one. It's an estate car and a woman's driving it. From this distance I can't be entirely sure but I rather fancy I've met her before.'

Magda had stopped the car and had left it, walking towards the hut with some caution. She was probably armed, Charles Russell decided, but if so she wasn't showing her weapon. He opened the door and called to her in the only language they had in common:

'*Avanti*. You're very welcome indeed.'

She greeted him with a certain formality, appropriate in Gael Milo's emissary, but also with an evident warmth. Charles Russell introduced Dick Bentinck. 'He has the advantage of me. He speaks your language.'

'That's no advantage. Not when it matters.'

Richard Bentinck bowed and began to talk to her. She was pleased but not unduly impressed.

'This gentleman'—Bentinck waved at the *jäger*—'is our hospitable and remarkable host.'

'I've heard of him. He's a burnt-out funny.'

Bentinck translated this comment succinctly, using a very American word. Charles Russell who was tolerant of many things besides horrible smells gave no sign that he had understood him.

'Come and help me unload the car,' Magda said.

The three of them unloaded the car while the *jäger* stood aside, indifferent. There were provisions for at least a week, eggs and fresh meat ('You don't need an icebox up here in the mountains, you put things out at night instead') flour and butter and most of the country's vegetables. There was also a crate of beer and some whisky. Finally two stoves to cook on.

They put these spoils in the cabin's lean-to and Russell helped Magda to wash two tables. She said with a hint of her first embarrassment:

'I'm sorry that there's no bacon or pork—I know all Englishmen love to eat them. That's prejudice left over from childhood.'

'The prejudice is perfectly sound. I eat bacon in England and in parts of America, which doesn't include the Southern States. Also in Holland and northern Germany. But almost anywhere else it's excessively dangerous. I caught a tapeworm once. I don't mean to again.'

'You're a sensible man. I like men sensible.'

'That's the best news I've had since I came to this country.'

Russell pumped up both stoves and Magda lit them. The lean-to by now was in very fair order, as a kitchen not up to those plugged in the glossies but well capable of producing food. Magda looked round it with satisfaction.

'Anything more I can do?' Russell asked.

'Nothing whatever.'

'In that case I'll go.'

'Don't do that—stay and watch me.' She had said it but with less than conviction.

'Two women in one kitchen is hell.'

Magda began to laugh uninhibitedly. She did it as she did most things, with gusto. Her fine bosom shook, her bold eyes ran. 'You're experienced as well as sensible.'

'One day I would hope to prove it.'

'Not on duty. It is not allowed.'

Charles Russell went back to the living-room thoughtfully. By four in the afternoon it was cold and the *jäger* had made up the fire in the grate. He was sitting by it in total silence, explicable since even Magda had no word of a language he understood. His manner was still a polite acceptance but his opinion of women was very clear. If Milo chose to send him friends that was something which he would meet as a duty, but sending a woman too was bad taste. He sat on in a sort of courteous sulk.

The whisky had been left in the living-room and as the evening darkened the three men used it. Russell went back to the lean-to to offer one, a little uncertain how Magda would take it. He needn't have worried, she accepted it gladly, laughing and reading his private doubt shrewdly. 'You were thinking that since I don't eat pork I might not accept a drink as well. I told you that that was only prejudice and secretly I'm a little ashamed of it. But I learnt to drink in my time in the army—plum brandy and I didn't much like it. But all the other girls drank so I drank too.'

'This isn't plum brandy.'

'I like it much better.'

It was dark when she brought in the meal to the table. Basically it was kebabs and rice, and Russell had eaten it often and badly, in Cypriot restaurants struggling in London, in Turkish hotels where the smell of the plumbing pervaded even the tarted-up dining-room. But this one was good with long thin rice, each grain quite separate. There were pieces of aubergine, a hint of red peppers, the latter chopped up, as it should be, small. The meat on the skewers was chicken and liver. Charles Russell said:

'This is very good.'

'I'm happy you like it. I cooked it with love.'

He didn't comment on this since unsure of her meaning. Her Italian was much less than perfect, and in any case the simple statement could bear one of two meanings and maybe both. All good cooks cooked with love, the love of their craft, but she had given him generous hints already and when the time came Charles Russell would take them up. He hoped that that time would not be protracted.

They were sitting in the cosy glow of the *jäger's* two old-fashioned oil lamps. The fire had begun to smoke but not badly. Russell and Bentinck were drinking beer, the *jäger* his own thin acid wine. It was a comfortable domestic scene and Russell pushed his chair back happily.

He was lighting his after dinner cigar when the window

crashed in in a shower of glass. A second later they heard the machine pistol's chatter.

All four of them went under the table.

There was a moment of numb and silent astonishment, then Russell took charge by simple instinct. 'Automatic, that was,' he said. 'That's bad.'

'You mean he'll work closer and take us sitting?' It was Bentinck; he sounded concerned but calm.

'That's just what I mean. Or he'll throw a grenade. He will, that is, if we don't get him first.'

'That girl's got a hand gun. I'll borrow it.'

'Useless.'

'There's that rifle above the fireplace.'

'I know.'

'I'll go,' Bentinck said.

Russell answered by gesture, pointing at Magda. Magda was already crawling, inching her way towards the fireplace. At it she stood, a second's target, and instantly there was another burst. It shot out both lamps and the *jäger* grunted. Magda was down again, under the table. She also had the *jäger's* rifle. She began to talk to Richard Bentinck, using her own language urgently.

'She says she's going to stalk him.'

'Excellent. If there's more than one man we've had it in any case, but if he's alone he can't watch all sides. Behind here is where our host grows his vegetables and at the bottom is a hedge and a ha-ha. If she can get into that she's a very fair chance. I have reason,' Charles Russell added coolly, 'to have confidence in this splendid lady.'

'We can't send a girl on a grown man's job. I've been trained you know.'

'You've already proved it. But in a rifle against an auto-

matic? In country you don't know? With a half moon?
Have you ever stalked an animal?'

'No.'

'Then swallow your pride as I'm eating my age.'

While they'd been talking Magda had left them. She'd
slipped out through the lean-to: they hadn't heard her.
She had left her Lüger by Russell's side.

'If neither of us is up to the job then maybe we should
have sent the *jäger*.'

'No,' Russell said.

'Why not?'

'He's dead.'

They lay there with the *jäger*'s body. Two minutes went
by, then three, then five.

'He's not hurrying,' Bentinck said.

'Why should he? But he's shot out the lamps—that
goes against him. Evidently he's not a professional—
browning blind into a room like that. But we've got to
assume he isn't stupid. What moon there is is right behind him and if he shows near the window we might be
armed. As it happens we are.' Russell picked up the Lüger.
'The lady left this—extremely thoughtful.' He was covering the window steadily.

'I don't like it,' Bentinck said.

'Nor do I.'

'If there was something we could do——'

'There isn't.'

There was another burst of staccato fire.

'That sounded further away.'

'It was.'

'What's happening?' Bentinck asked.

Russell frowned. 'It's a long time since I did infantry
training but it was a sound principle to draw enemy fire.

That is, when you didn't know where they were.'

'You mean she's been exposing herself—trying to spot him by the flash of his weapon?'

'How else could she hope to pick him up? When the moon's behind cloud it's as dark as the pit.'

'I don't like it,' Bentinck said again. 'He could easily catch her first.'

'Not so easily.'

They lay in the darkness, anxious and tense. The fire had diminished, the window had fallen, and already the cold was seeping in. The *jäger*'s body had started to stiffen but the two live men had begun to sweat. When the moon came out from behind the cloud there was a fickle light at the broken window. Russell continued to cover it steadily.

They heard another burst from the automatic. It seemed neither closer nor further away.

'He didn't get her the first time,' Bentinck said grimly.

'I don't think he's going to get her at all.' Russell was silent, then added quietly: 'I like that girl, I really do.' He had spoken conversationally and Bentinck was left unsure of the message.

'Do you think that man is going to chance it? When he knows there's someone after him he might risk a rush at the hut to finish us.'

Charles Russell shook an experienced head. 'As I said, we mustn't assume he's stupid. On three sides of this cabin it's open ground, as much as forty yards in places. That's why he opened fire as he did. I know there's a hedge and a garden behind, but I don't think he'd try to break in through the lean-to. If he'd had a grenade he'd have used it by now but most amateurs are scared stiff of grenades. So he'll have to deal first with whoever is after him, then he'll lie in close cover and use his fire power. He can't penetrate this cabin's logs, but he'll be shooting through the window and downwards. He only needs enough ammunition and sooner or later he's bound to get us. Probably,' Russell added, 'by ricochet. That's how he got that unfortunate *jäger*.'

There was a third burst from the scrub above them. Richard Bentinck said: 'That was very much closer.'

For a moment the moon had cleared the cloud and Russell crawled across to the window. He raised himself and peered out cautiously. Almost at once he ducked decisively.

'You were right—the man's closing. I saw a movement on the edge of the scrub.'

'That means he's got the girl.'

'Or thinks so.'

'What do we do?'

'There's little we can. We'll both of us watch—different sides of the window. We'll be targets but he's not a marksman. Once he starts firing get down at once. I've an idea where he is and I might be lucky.' Russell looked at the Lüger. '*Very* lucky. It's twenty-five yards and I'm not in practice.'

Outside there was a single shot, the unmistakable crack of a rifle.

'So he didn't get the girl.'

'Praise God. Also it changes the situation. Knowing that she's still behind him he can't stay where he is and brown us down. He'll have to rush us and he's not a pro. He'll rush us and he'll rush us firing.'

'Much good that will do us.'

'It might do a little. I will offer you a hundred to eight. For a man who presumably isn't an athlete, firing from a sling and slowed by it, twenty-five yards will be fully four seconds. When the firing starts I'll count three and then chance it. If the moon goes in I haven't a hope or he may cut me in half before I can sight.'

'You could give me the pistol,' Dick Bentinck said.

'I could and I don't doubt you're better with it. Just the same I'm not going to.'

'Okay.'

They were standing on opposite sides of the window, exposing their heads in alternation as they stared into the still clear moonlight. It was Bentinck who said:

'He's coming.'

He came. Both men had dropped and Russell said: 'One.' The stream of fire through the broken window was a foot above the lying men but it was tearing the *jäger's* hut to pieces. The floor was cement and the angle changing, debris and dust were flying wickedly. Occasionally, as a round struck metal, it whined ominously past their cringing bodies.

Russell said: 'Two.' He began to rise.

Through the stammer of the automatic they could both of them hear the second rifle shot. The automatic stopped firing suddenly. For a second the silence was worse than the uproar.

Magda had had one sighting and missed but she hadn't been used to the *jäger's* rifle. In her way she had been enjoying herself for she'd been taught to use cover and move at night and her instinct had been that her quarry had not. As Russell had thought she had drawn his fire, not too frightened that at fifty yards a man who was clearly not her equal would be able to hit her in fleeting moonlight. When she'd spotted his flash she knew that she had him, though once she had had to offer again when the moon went in cloud and she temporarily lost him.

She'd been astonished when he started moving, not to the end of some open clearing where his weapon would be a huge advantage, but back towards the hut itself. This, she decided, was over-confidence: he must be sure that his second burst had got her. A professional would have made quite sure, but it was evident and always had been that this man on the hill was not her match. She smiled, scenting duty completely accomplished. She wasn't a sadist, she didn't love killing, but she wouldn't have liked to have left undone what Gael Milo would have wished her to do. So once he started towards the hut she had him. If he stayed still she could stalk and kill him, and if he tried a rush over open ground he'd be a very easy target indeed.

When he made his rush she had dropped him first time.

Now she came out of the scrub with confidence, but with rifle still loaded and cocked and ready. She saw that she wouldn't need it again, then she rolled Bojalian's body over. What she saw for the first time that evening shook her. 'That one,' she said to herself. 'Astonishing.'

She walked back to the hut with the *jäger's* rifle, carrying it at the Rifleman's trail. Both men were at the door to meet her and characteristically Richard Bentinck spoke first.

'Did you know him?' he asked.

'I knew him all right.' She added with less than her usual clarity: 'Most of us knew what he was—what he did. Naturally I'll report his death. Someone will come and take him away.'

Richard Bentinck had started to speak but Charles Russell had cut in urbanely. There was something here concerned Magda alone and he didn't wish her cross-examined. 'Congratulations.' He took her hand.

'A pleasure,' she said.

'I shall try to repay you.'

'I hope you will find the repayment pleasant.'

'I haven't a doubt in the world of that.'

It was a happy and possibly fruitful exchange but Richard Bentinck had again interrupted. He didn't understand Italian, and though efficient and, when he had to be, ruthless, he wasn't a man of outstanding tact. He looked round the ruined hut.

'What now?'

'I have received my instructions for such an occasion.' Magda spoke with a stiff and offended formality.

'We must know what they are.'

She ignored him coldly, turning to Russell. 'If we met any kind of trouble here I was to take you to Gael Milo at once.'

'You're sure of that?'

'Of course I'm sure.' With Charles Russell she was entirely relaxed. 'She was going to bring you in in any case but she wanted to see that your flat was quite ready.' She laughed at him. 'You're very important.'

'I don't feel important, I feel quite useless.'

'I'm sure you're not that.'

'Not in some ways perhaps.'

But Bentinck had broken in again. He had the feeling he'd been a passenger and was anxious to reassert his competence.

'What's going on?'

Charles Russell translated.

'Do you think that's okay?'

'I think that's okay. In any case what choice do we have?' He pointed at the *jäger*'s rifle. He had already given back Magda's Lüger.

Richard Bentinck didn't give up easily. 'There are loose ends here. We ought to tidy them.'

'If you're thinking of the man outside somebody else will be coming for that one. I agree about the *jäger*, though. We can't just leave him to rot on the floor.' Charles Russell turned again to Magda. 'How deep is that ha-ha?'

'Say half a metre.'

'We'll put him in there. There's a spade in the lean-to and earth in the garden. It shouldn't take more than twenty minutes.' A thought struck him and he put it to Magda. 'I suppose that man outside was alone?'

'Knowing who he was I'm sure of it.'

'Good.'

They carried the *jäger* out and buried him. Russell asked Magda: 'Do you know his religion?'

'Most of the people round here are Christian.' She spoke less with contempt than a real regret.

They returned to the hut and Russell looked round it. There was an object which he'd already noticed, a carving in cherrywood, lovingly done. It was a very beautiful thing indeed; it was also an extreme of obscenity. Russell put it in his pocket quietly. 'If he's got any heirs I'll return it at once. Alternatively I'll try and buy it.'

Magda said with surprise: 'You like such things?'

'I assure you that's not my personal taste. It just happens to be extremely good.'

'Very well. And if you're ready we'll go.'

'Just a moment, please.' Russell went to the lean-to. He'd seen a couple of planks and found hammer and nails. He tacked the planks together roughly, borrowing Magda's torch to do it. Then he wrote on the cross in his bold clear scrawl:

A HAPPY MAN

Requiescat in Pace

He stuck the cross in the soil by the *jäger's* head, saying
the only prayer he remembered. Then he went back to the
car and the others. He was feeling a little sheepish but
satisfied.

11

There was a tradition that very senior soldiers might speak with a certain bluntness but the General was too civilized to employ this manner when speaking to Gael. He couldn't say to her: 'When your husband dies,' but he'd contrived to convey that his interest lay in the period after Milo's death. Gael Milo had understood him perfectly. She was in no way resentful but pleased he had called on her. Like herself he was a solid Southerner.

Nevertheless, despite his tact, he was a professional soldier and liked the facts clear. 'I'm troubled about the future,' he said.

She decided she would have to help him. 'When Milo drops the reins, you mean?'

'Precisely that.'

'So are most of our people.'

'Who hold, as you know, the real military power, but politically they're one of three."

'Isn't it early to talk about fighting?'

'It depends,' he said, 'what sort of fighting.' He accepted her coffee, a cigarette. 'Kamich is the heir apparent.'

'You mistrust him?'

'Profoundly.'

'And so do I. But I don't believe he's an active traitor.'

He began to recite and in much the same terms what an ambassador had already told her. 'I don't think he'd openly sell us East but equally he wouldn't stand pressure. He *couldn't* stand pressure—not with his background. It would come on quite soon and it would come on increasingly. Kamich is not the man to resist it.'

She wondered how much this soldier knew, the army had its own Intelligence. He possibly didn't know of the gold but he might know about Bojalian's death. She decided to feel him out obliquely.

'Do you know of any particular reason why the pressure should start before Milo retires?'

'No,' the General said, 'I do not.'

... So he doesn't know but he does have a right to. If those others take action he ought to know why. Soldiers in blinkers are worse than useless.

She told him about Bojalian's death and the General allowed a muted whistle. 'How long before they find out?' he asked.

'It might be a week—we've removed the body. But they'll notice quite soon that he's broken off contact—the unofficial contact, that is—and since he hasn't been attending his embassy his ambassador has told the police. They won't find him and nor will anyone else.'

'How do you think it will go?'

'At first?' Gael shrugged but she was privately certain. 'At first there'll be a furious protest, then one of our men will be rudely expelled on some trumped-up charge of running a spy ring. At the worst they might even break off relations.'

The General said quietly: 'No more than that?'

'What had you in mind?'

'Their moving troops to the frontier.'

'Wouldn't that be an over-reaction?'

'To the death of a man like Bojalian—yes.'

'Then what are you thinking of?'

'A rumour.'

Gael Milo was not entirely surprised. So this General hadn't known of Bojalian but he'd heard a whisper of something much more important. 'A rumour,' he was saying again.

'Do you wish to discuss that rumour?'

'Unnecessary. And not my business. The fact that it exists is enough.'

'To justify their moving troops?'

'They might think so.'

'And what would you do if they did?'

'Move mine.' He held up a hand as she started to speak. 'You mustn't misunderstand me, though. I flatter myself that we're very well trained but we couldn't delay them for more than ten days. After that we'd be in the mountains again and neither of us wishes that for a moment.'

'What are you advising, General?'

'I have permission to speak freely?'

'Certainly.'

'It's essential to avoid an internal power struggle.'

'And how do we do that?'

'With Kamich.'

'But I heard you say——'

He stopped her firmly. 'I chose the preposition with care. Not "by" Kamich or even "through" him. I said "with" and I meant it. I mean it still.'

'I'm not sure I follow.'

'It's basically simple. We're agreed that he'd make too many concessions—he'd be obliged to make too many concessions. But Kamich has a single advantage: as the heir apparent he formally is he could pick up the reins with comparative smoothness.'

'He wouldn't last long,' Gael Milo said grimly.

The General drew a long breath and released it. 'There are circumstances in which he might.'

'What circumstances?'

'With a powerful ally.'

'You're suggesting the army would back him?'

'Never. I'm suggesting the army would back yourself.'

Gael Milo was silent, thinking hard. She had heard this before as an abstract proposal: an ambassador had promised approval. But this was more than a promise of general approval, it was a concrete offer of concrete help and from a source which she could trust, her own people. When the ambassador had taken his leave she had gone to her office and picked up the telephone. Then she had put it down again, her political fences were not worth mending. She was a member of the People's House and thirty others would probably follow her. That wasn't a power base.

The army was.

She said to the General: 'You want an alliance?'

'Call it that or anything else you please. In the simplest terms I want Kamich in, but only because that's the simplest way to avoid what might tear the country to pieces, perhaps even start a civil war which my duty it would be to crush. But once he's in I want him policed. That's a brutal word and you may not like it, but also he's going to need support if he intends to stand up to our evident enemies. You have the name and prestige to give it, to shackle one hand but give power to the other.'

Gael said with a perfectly candid doubt: 'There's only thirty or so who would follow me certainly.'

'In the People's House? That is now irrelevant. Madam, I am no politician. I'm not promising you a block of votes.'

'You may not be a politician but I think you're a very intelligent man.'

For the first time the General permitted a smile. 'There's a tradition in my strange profession that soldiers shouldn't play with politics. It is sound but it has a great disadvantage. It often makes us seem very stupid, much stupider than in fact we are.'

'If Kamich and I went in double harness, call it Joint Premiers, what you will—if Kamich should agree to that what guarantee has he or I that we don't just become the army's puppets?'

'You don't have any guarantee except the facts which can speak for themselves. If I wanted to be a common dictator I shouldn't be here and talking to you. I should be *wanting* chaos, maybe stirring it up. The army may not be strong enough to hold a major Power for more than ten days but it's something more than capable of declaring martial law and enforcing it.'

'I think,' she said slowly, 'I'll have to trust you.'

'Excellent. We can work out the details.' He rose and kissed her hand but waited. He had something more to convey. It was delicate. He said finally: 'Time is a serious factor now.'

'You're thinking of my husband's health?'

'These crises can arrive very suddenly. With your permission I shall stay in the capital.'

'But you won't move in tanks?'

'Of course I shall not.' He added with a crisp asperity: 'You were kind enough to tell me before that you didn't think me entirely stupid. I shall do nothing foolish and nothing provocative. Just the same I shall stay here. And at your service.' He put on his cap and saluted formally. 'At the service of Milo's wife,' he said.

He walked back to his quarters smiling contentedly. He didn't consider his morning wasted. He realized that what he'd proposed to Gael Milo wouldn't strike her as anything strange or abnormal. She was a Southerner as he was himself, and in their vigorous, sometimes violent country widows would often stand in for their husbands, managing the family farm till the sons reached an age to take it over. The family, he'd have agreed, was everything— everything good but everything bad. He personally disapproved of the blood feud but he couldn't deny it a secret respect. He himself preferred the rule of law, but in a country of great territorial magnates where cattle and land were still king and queen the rule of law could be often bent. It had been bent in his own village last year, and as it happened it was a widow who'd straightened it. Everyone knew who'd killed her husband but he was wealthy and also the local mayor and the judge had refused to admit as evidence what in any normal case he would have. The sons were only children still so the widow had gone to the killer's house with her husband's shotgun loaded with buckshot. When he'd opened she'd fired at his face point blank. It had happened in the afternoon but nobody had seen a thing, there wasn't a single witness available. There was a sort of wild justice in that perhaps, whatever more delicate minds might make of it.

The General checked this musing sharply. Whatever now happened to Milo's widow it was very unlikely to come to that. Milo was going to die quite soon but with reasonable luck he would die in his bed.

The General had talked of a sudden crisis but Kamich's was on him already. Bojalian hadn't been seen for three days and already, as Foreign Minister, Kamich was being put to the question by phone calls and by ponderous Notes whose tone was increasingly sharp and menacing. The fact that he could guess what had happened in no way decreased his official problem. He'd sent men to Milo's hut in the mountains who'd reported that it had been wrecked by gunfire. Its tenant had been decently buried but of Bojalian there wasn't a sign or trace. Kamich would have agreed with Gael Milo: moving troops to the frontier would be an over-reaction, or an over-reaction to Bojalian's death, but Kamich knew something which Gael did not. The masters of those troops, through Bojalian, had made him a final proposition; they had called it a very generous offer but Kamich knew well how these men's minds worked. And the answer to that proposition had been the disappearance of the man who had brought it. The two events were not strictly connected—Bojalian himself had triggered the second—but it would be reasonable to assume they were. The people whom Kamich was thinking of were prickly and very conscious of power. At best they would see this as ill-timed impertinence; at the worst they would see it as open defiance, as a gage thrown down to mark future policy.

In which case they might act at once.

Kamich was on the horns and knew it. He saw that he must now seize power; he must take it before it vanished for ever, destroyed by a totally ruthless enemy.

He began to think as he'd always been taught to, in terms of the political facts. The North wouldn't back him —certainly not. The North had the industry, much higher incomes, and Milo had always ridden it on a rein which Kamich thought much too loose. It was one of the reasons Kamich mistrusted him, he'd been liberal, a dirty word. Why, the North even had Trade Unions and those

Trade Unions a share of real power. Such a people wouldn't back Kamich. Never. Not that that greatly mattered now for the North was not a fighting people, but it would matter after he came to power. There might even be a general strike. Then he'd crush out these liberal heresies firmly. Trade Union bosses grown suave and sleek—there were more ways of dealing with men like that than letting them hold the country to ransom.

His own Central Province, then? He frowned. Unquestionably it would support him blindly but in a pinch that support would be worth very little, just a block of votes in the People's House which in a crisis would sink into total impotence. The Central Province had neither the North's new industries nor the power of the South to raise the clans, only its own fierce independence, dour peasants who took to the mountains and waited. Kamich sighed for he both loved these people and also in a sense he despised them. Dour peasants who sat out invasions grimly but also peasants who wanted release for their children. So they educated them into unemployment. The capital was full of them, aping western fashions in dress and hair, marching with banners, always protesting, a sickness from perfectly healthy stock which any communist must detest on principle. They should be protesting against their parents' ambitions, not the actions of great Powers in the East.

Kamich rose from his desk and looked out of the window. It was clear that he'd have to concede an alliance, and if the North wouldn't help him and the Centre couldn't, that left only the South and they weren't his friends. They had a very well organized vote in the House, but the three or four men who managed it would reject an advance from Kamich contemptuously. Then go to the army? They'd do the same. But the South was a strange uncontemporary country; there were even people who called it feudal. What mattered in it were family loyalties, your standing in the community, name. Gael Milo, Kamich thought—she had all of them.

Once she had owned substantial power, both through her mother's name and personally. In her own right she had been a politician, sufficiently influential, too, to bring Milo the South as a private dowry. She'd let most of that go in a happy marriage, but she still had her name and her mother's mystique. Was she ambitious? He didn't know. If she were it might somehow just be on. For a time, for the time that he needed Gael Milo. When he held the reins firmly he'd quietly ditch her.

Or wouldn't he? he wondered suddenly. She was, after all, a dazzling woman. An alliance, if he brought it off, might have advantages besides the political.

He disciplined this thinking sharply. It was something in a possible future but for the moment the problem was more precise. It was premature to think of allies when no alliance was even possible so long as Milo stayed in the saddle. The medical reports suggested that he wasn't going to die tomorrow but clearly he'd never return again as the Old Master who'd held the country together. One day he'd quietly fade away but Kamich couldn't wait for that. He couldn't because he knew others who mightn't.

Milo's death would have to be, well, accelerated.

He began to consider the act dispassionately. Trained as he had been he thought impersonally. He had failed once in London when under pressure but now the pressure was ten times greater. Now it wasn't a question of reaching power but of reaching it within days, even hours, before disaster struck at his country finally. Words like killing and murder were contemptibly bourgeois.

He picked a report from his desk and re-read it. Those students were going to riot again, parading in the main square with banners, chanting, throwing stones and bottles, an offence to all right-thinking citizens. And Milo would kid-glove them again, another entry in the long score against him. Kamich would have sent in the riot police and if that hadn't worked he'd have shot without scruple, but Milo would use the ordinary police and with orders to be unprovocative. Unprovocative! These scenes were an outrage. The police would link arms in lines and suffer, sweating it out under spittle and insult. Where did Milo believe he was living—in London? Then, when the foolish fury was cooling, he'd walk out onto the palace's balcony. He'd raise his arms in that actor's gesture and as often as not they would quieten and listen. It wasn't what he said, which was pap, but the fact that this was Milo, hearing them. There were people who said his charisma was fading. It was still an extremely potent weapon.

So he'd come onto the balcony, he'd come out there and he'd be standing alone. Milo would never shoot. Kamich must.

12

Charles Russell looked round the little flat, the quarters for very private guests. Gael's aunts from the South had sometimes stayed here or Milo's hard brothers come down from the North. There was a bedroom, a sitting-room, tiny kitchen, where Magda came in daily to cook for him. She had a room of her own along the corridor. The view was across the formal garden, and though the climate prevented English-style gardening the thirsty beds were clean and weeded, the hedges clipped and the paths well rolled. The statues were vaguely Greek and playful.

Charles Russell was now alone and glad of it. After violence he'd always reacted strongly and he wouldn't have wished to discuss it with Bentinck, frustrated and restless and eager for action. He was happy that Bentinck had quietly gone: one day he'd been there and the next he had not. His departure had not surprised Charles Russell for he knew how Bentinck's world would work. He'd been useful as a listening ear and useful in the preliminary violence which was the overture to larger events; he'd been brave and within his limits resourceful but he wouldn't be seeing the end of the play. Charles Russell had liked him and wished him well. He would end, he decided, as some sort of desk man, a senior and respected desk man but not one who was allowed near policy. So they'd recalled him and wouldn't send another, or if they did he would be very different. The crisis in this explosive state had moved well ahead of the Richard Bentincks.

So Russell was content to relax, knowing from a lifetime's experience that there were times when inaction, a quiet passivity, were the only forms of practical wisdom. To try to force a crisis was mostly fatal, it would come when the gods' sense of drama demanded it. He had books and newspapers, comfortable quarters, and Magda was trying to teach him her language. But it was a pity she was quite so punctilious. 'Never on duty,' she'd said and she'd meant it.

A knock on the door interrupted breakfast and when Russell opened it Gael came in. He had seen her twice since Magda had brought him here and each time he had thought her increasingly strained. Today she had fought to a sort of repose and Charles Russell could sense she had made a decision. From her manner it might be a very big one but she wasn't yet ready to discuss it with Russell. Instead she said:

'I've come to offer an explanation. It was I who told Richard Bentinck's ambassador who was hiding him and where and why.'

'I think that was a wise thing to do.'

She hesitated. 'I spoke to yours too.'

But Charles Russell nodded. 'Also sensible.'

'You don't resent it?'

'Why ever should I? I'm not important enough to rate formal protest but Commonwealth may have been sending messages——'

'They have,' she said, and she opened her bag. 'This came for you care of the British embassy. They were to find you within four days or report it.'

Charles Russell took the envelope, wrestling with the

heavy seals. Gael smiled and passed him her mother's knife. She'd been carrying it in her bag as usual. Russell knew that she was proud of it, flattered that she had even lent it.

He slit the envelope and gave back the knife, reading his letter, frowning, deciding. 'It's from Commonwealth as I thought,' he said. 'They want me to go back at once.'

'And will you?' she asked.

'That depends on you.'

'I don't think that's fair—you're quite free to leave. Just the same I would like you to stay a while.' Nostalgia was not a word which Charles Russell would have hung on Gael but for a moment she was almost nostalgic. 'My mother told me you're not my father but I never knew the man who was. The Germans got him before I was born. Like it or not you're a father substitute.'

'I'm honoured but I'm not very useful here.'

'It's just that I'm happy to have you behind me.' She hesitated again, then told him. 'Milo's sinking, you know?'

'You mean he's dying?'

'No, I don't think he's dying, or not so you see it, but he'll never again be what he was.'

Russell said softly: 'The reins are slipping?'

'They're slipping towards what we none of us like.'

Since she thought him a surrogate father he chanced it. 'And you've taken a major decision?'

'Yes.'

'Is that why you've come to see me?'

'Yes again.'

'Then hadn't you better tell me?'

'No.'

Charles Russell didn't ask: 'Why not?' but accepted the contradiction calmly. There were men who claimed to read women's signals but Charles Russell had seldom attempted to do so. He was content to like women, that they mostly liked him. But of course it was wise to observe their backgrounds. Gael Milo's had been characteristic and he didn't believe that she'd ever outgrown it.... The South, the blazing explosive South. Brave and handsome men and gorgeous women and underneath a near barbarity, instant violence and the ancestral feud. Blood must be always repaid in blood.

So he didn't presume to understand her but he knew something which the too-clever did not. Women, if pressed, gave you hatfuls of reasons, but the real one, if they knew it, they hid. What was important was very different: when they'd decided on something they mostly did it.

When Kamich had called the student up he'd been surprised but not entirely astonished. For he wasn't one of the futile protesters, unemployable by his country's industry which suspected them, often rightly, of silliness, and unemployed by the state which paid his fees since the North had its own longstanding stranglehold on any work in his country's civil service. The arrogance of the average student he despised as much as did Kamich himself, who had noticed him for what he was, completely committed to one philosophy, the essential Party man of the future. He'd been promised a job when he got his degree, the kind of work he would wish to have, not a well paid job since very few were, but work where he could stretch his muscles and with any luck achieve his ambitions. Kamich had noticed these as well. This boy wanted power and meant to have it: more important he would do most things to get it. Wasting time in vague protests—lost causes, nonstarters? He spent his leisure in reading, in more than one language, how the men of new countries had come to rule them, and one thing he had learnt already. Before you could rule you would have to serve.

He was ready to do it and was now being asked to, secretly flattered that Kamich had chosen him. Kamich had other and better-trained followers but few had this boy's dedication and many might well refuse this order. If Kamich chose wrong and the man betrayed him he wouldn't live longer than three or four hours. Milo might not be the Master he had been but he was still in the saddle, his writ still ran.

So Kamich was telling the student now, very much man to man, very serious: 'So you see how it is and it just won't do. Whatever it is in these mountains of ours Milo has sold it out to the West.'

The boy said earnestly: 'The act of a traitor.'

'And time is an essential factor. The people who think like you and me can reach power if Milo doesn't linger. But if he does then the army and maybe the North ...' Kamich's shrug was expressively eloquent.

'What do you want me to do?'

Kamich told him.

The boy thought it over, excited but careful. 'Suppose Milo doesn't come out on the balcony?'

'Milo will.' He was sure of it. Milo had never used the riot police. Kamich would have sent them in with orders to hand out a wholesome lesson and if that hadn't worked he'd have fired unhesitatingly. But Milo would simply go out and talk; Milo was soft as a rotten orange.

'I can't shoot from a crowd of other students.'

'Of course you can't—that's all been arranged. There'll be a room in the office opposite, a clear sighting across the heads of the crowd. The rifle will be waiting there—I'll attend to all the details myself. Then you wipe it clean and slip down to the crowd. Remember that you're a student yourself. You'll no more be suspect than hundreds of others.'

'And if something goes wrong?'

'What could go wrong?'

'Somebody standing just below me.... They could hear the shot from above very well.... They come rushing upstairs before I get down....'

Kamich was in his fashion honest. 'Then I'm afraid you'd be out on your own. Alone.'

'But I shouldn't be quite alone.'

'Why not?'

The boy said with a touch of dignity: 'I'm not a hero and I haven't been trained. The police could persuade me to talk. Very quickly.'

'The police would grill you but not beat you up.' Kamich had spoken with total conviction for the rules for interrogation were stringent. It was another decision he held against Milo, an obeisance to the decadent West. Once it had been notably otherwise but Milo had chosen to change all that. At first the police had not believed him—this was window-dressing for foreign approval—but one Commissioner had been quietly removed, another publicly broken and sent to prison. 'They won't torture you,' Kamich said.

'You're sure.'

'If I wasn't I know I'd be risking my life.'

The boy thought it over: the argument bit. 'Very well,' he said. 'When is it?'

'Tonight.'

Magda had brought Charles Russell supper and now

joined him in the dusty garden. The garden lay away from the square but the increasing noise of a crowd filtered through to them. Magda said in her bad Italian:

'I'm frightened.'

'That's something I've never seen you before. You're frightened of a mob of students?'

'Not of them. I'm frightened for them.'

'Why?'

'Well, what do you do in England?'

He laughed. 'In England we're what's called permissive. We send out the police to link arms and suffer. They're abused and often worse than that.'

'That's silly,' she said.

'There are people who think so.'

'What do you think yourself?'

'I don't know. I don't think I'd do what the French do, for instance—send in riot police who know how to hurt and do. That strikes me as counter-productive or worse.'

'But if the riot became serious, if the crowd started stoning?'

'There's gas and there are rubber bullets.' He added with very real contempt: 'Soldiers firing rubber bullets! It isn't what they're paid to do, it isn't even fair to ask them.'

'You'd use real ones then?'

'That's not my decision.'

'But if they ordered you?'

'I'd obey my orders.'

'Milo would never do that,' she said. 'He loves those children. I think they smell.'

Milo was listening now, uneasy, a stricken man whose powers were fading. He was sitting in the enormous stateroom whose balcony overlooked the square; he'd seen this before and had always felt equal to it. Now he was undecided, uncertain. Gael was standing by the chair he sat in, holding a phone on a long lead of flex. He had only to take it: the noise would stop. There were mounted police at call and ready. He said wearily to his wife:

'Who are they?'

'All of them, and as usual divided. Some have banners about the war in Vietnam; some want more money; and all want work.'

'I can't find them work,' he said. 'I regret it.'

His wife didn't answer; she knew her own mind. These were pampered and over-privileged children, the state paid their fees to escape from their fields. But which of them had fought for his freedom, lying out in the mountains, half starved and frozen, risking death and quite often much worse than that? Why should they seek to leave their fields where their Christian God had seen fit to put them? They weren't like the young of Gael's own country who took to the army as a matter of course, content to serve and proud to do so, insisting only on their grandfathers' regiments; they weren't even like the boys of the North with their own grim university town. There students really worked and competed. No wonder they found themselves jobs—they deserved them. Kamich's people, she thought. She despised them.

She looked at her husband; he seemed to be sleeping. She nudged him with the telephone and he woke with something quite close to a groan. A decision which would once have come easily now demanded an unnatural effort.

'How does it go?'

'They're getting noisier.'

A bottle came through the wide french windows. The

glass sprayed across the parquet, but harmlessly. That should settle it, Gael thought.

It did not. Instead he began to rise but fell back again. 'Give me your arm,' he said. 'I must talk to them.' It had always worked before. It must now.

'You can't do it,' she said but she didn't say more. To tell him he wasn't the man he had been would destroy him more surely than any bottle.

'I can if you help me. Give me your hand.'

In the garden the noise of the crowd was growing and Magda had begun to fidget. Charles Russell said quietly: 'What are your orders? Have you orders to keep me away from what's happening?'

'Not expressly,' she said.

'Then I'd like to see.'

She led him through the palace quickly, through passages mostly unused and the kitchens, up a winding stone staircase, a green baize door. Beyond it was a carpeted corridor which ended in a fine bronze door. On the other side was the great reception room with its balcony onto the seething square.

Milo was in his wheel chair and frowning. Suddenly one of his tantrums took him. His face contorted but not in pain. This wasn't an act, it was genuine, frightening. 'The bastards,' he said. 'I'll show them still.'

He held out his arm but his wife ignored it. 'You can't do that. Lie down. Try to sleep.'

For answer he held out the other arm. She took them and pulled him slowly upright. She was supporting him but only just. She'd obeyed since a wife was beholden to do so but it was the first time Charles Russell had seen her weeping. She opened the long french windows reluctantly.

Russell and Magda had crept up behind them. Magda said something but Gael didn't answer. She was out on the balcony now, holding Milo.

He raised his arms and began to speak but the magic had all too clearly flown. He had done this before and indeed it had worked, by the power of his superlative oratory, by his deep strong voice, by his huge personality. Now the voice was the pipe of an ageing man, the oratory incoherent mumble. He raised his arms again, seeking silence, not getting it. There was a storm of insensate booing, blind anger, then the noise of the crowd went down a half-tone.

Charles Russell, wise in the ways of crowds, took Milo by the coat-sleeve firmly. He was expecting a shower of stones and worse.

The first shot lodged in Milo's stomach. He collapsed but Russell was holding him now. For an instant there was an appalling silence, then the second shot whined past Russell's shoulder.

The third went into Milo's head.

Charles Russell carried him back to the stateroom, laying him on an Empire sofa. He didn't need to look at him. Milo, the Old Master, was dead.

Leaving one, he thought later, and he too was mortal.

13

The American ambassador had received further and even more urgent instructions. He also considered them even sillier, though for once they had also been explicit. Mid Western, an American company, was now in effect in control of Commonwealth by a purchase of shares by private arrangement, and Commonwealth held the sole concession for mining this all-important gold. There was a vital American interest here and His Excellency must fight for it hard.

The dispatch began to explain the reasons but the ambassador skimmed them, smiling dryly. He could visualize the man who had drafted them, some bright young academic economist, and he knew what he needed to know already. Since Bretton Woods had at last collapsed monetary gold was at thirty-eight dollars and looking very sick at that. To talk of the dollar being devalued was something one wasn't encouraged to do, but the fact remained it was now inconvertible and at thirty-eight dollars no central bank was willing in practice to part with its gold. The free market price had touched eighty yesterday and South Africa, very sensibly, was holding back nearly half her production. Russia too for the moment was not in the market but it took only about three tons of gold to move its price by a dollar an ounce.

All that, the ambassador thought, was interesting, but

it hadn't yet touched the essential point. The relationship between the official price and a price in a market nominally free but seemingly being starved deliberately was something for the bankers to handle, and since they made themselves comfortable incomes by doing so the ambassador thought that they probably would. What was dangerous was something different, that an uncovenanted new supply would fall into enemy hands and be used by them. The ambassador would not have been angered if he'd been called a somewhat old-fashioned man so he wasn't embarrassed to use the word enemy. He believed their objectives were still unchanged and such a weapon would be exploited ruthlessly. This gold would not be used responsibly to increase the fund of credit available and so grease the wheels of costive trade; it would be used in some sudden and well planned attack against positions already sadly weakened. His Excellency didn't know the means but he didn't doubt the final end, the destruction of the capitalist system. This new gold could be a time bomb ticking, threatening the whole western world. In the end it might bring it tumbling down more effectively than communist takeovers.

The tone of the dispatch began to change. The economist was off the field and very much heavier metal was firing. And firing, the ambassador sensed, with a hint of a panic he much deplored. Panic was a very poor counsellor and the instructions which he was reading contemptuously were in his opinion simply stupid. With their premises he quite agreed: Milo had died and the pot was boiling; the senior Deputy Prime Minister had taken over under the constitution, but that meant little in itself or nothing and Kamich wouldn't last a week if he lost in the struggle for power now inevitable. The writer sincerely hoped he would but in the meantime he could do serious damage.

The ambassador didn't dissent from this but he thought his instructions were naive and dangerous. He was to call on Kamich and lean on him heavily; he was to talk about the arms for the army, the open aid and the secret subsidy. He was to make it plain these were gifts from the gods and the gods could be fickle as well as generous.

These were the ambassador's formal instructions and His Excellency ignored them blandly. Instead he put on his hat and called again on Gael Milo.

He found her in the palace still, calm by an effort but pleased to see him. He hadn't attended Milo's funeral since his wishes had been honoured scrupulously. He had forbidden any form of state funeral and had been buried in his native suburb on the fringe of a grim northern town. In theory he'd been a Lutheran and as a Lutheran they had dourly buried him. Only Gael and a handful of friends had been present.

The ambassador said: 'You've been under strain.' It was a statement of fact made without apology. 'If you'd rather not receive me now I can very well call again on you later.'

'But I'm always pleased to see my friends.'

He bowed. 'That's very generous.'

'No. And you once gave me very sage advice.'

'I remember we discussed a matter.' He left it at that and the next move to her. He was experienced and he wouldn't rush her.

But she followed it up, self-possessed and steady. He thought her a remarkable woman, calm in a crisis, dangerous if cornered. Well, she wasn't yet cornered—very far from it. 'I think your suggestion was perfectly practical but I don't think I could do it alone.'

'Alliances are always difficult. Alas that they are often necessary.'

161

'Politically, you mean? I might ride that. I was thinking of something much more personal.'

He guessed what she meant but let it pass. She was a very attractive woman still and the men of this country were undeniably male.

But she changed the subject. 'You said you could help us.'

He didn't comment on the plural. 'Yes?'

'It's a matter of Intelligence, whether yours, which is good, is the same as ours. Ours is that another country has made no movement of troops on or near our frontier.'

'Ours confirms that,' he said.

'If they did?'

'I cannot answer that directly. Moving troops against another's frontier is hardly the act of a friendly neighbour but it's a very long way short of war unless accompanied by an ultimatum. Undeniably it would be pressure politics, but that's a game for more than two. There'd be Notes and protests, counter pressures. Certainly by ourselves to start with. There would probably be a most dangerous period but I'd guess it would subside in the end.'

'If it didn't?' she asked. 'If it turned for the worse?'

'You're implying an invasion?'

She nodded.

He thought it over carefully, then answered with an old friend's candour. 'Only God can answer that question truthfully. To move troops to your frontiers would cause much commotion, the diplomats such as myself would lather, but an invasion would be of a different order, especially in view of our mutual interest. I very much dislike the cliché but it'd be eyeball to eyeball—little room for manoeuvre. And not only here—all over the world.

Whether our friends would face that at this moment is something which only they can tell you.'

'Thank you,' she said.

'At your service. I mean it.'

He rose and kissed her hand; he left her. He then went back home and changed his clothes; he changed into something much more formal. He had said that he was at her service and there was one which he could render at once. It would be wise to make the position explicit and he could do so across the heavy desk of a *cher collègue* who was not so dear.

He put it in diplomatic language but he made himself unmistakably clear. Any monkey business locally could not be confined to the local stage. It would be confrontation across the world.

He then went home and wrote a dispatch. He had received his instructions and had noted them carefully.

He poured himself a very large whisky; he felt that for once he had earned his money.

Gael's next visitor had called by appointment, bearing flowers and his most worldly manner. It was Kamich who had sought the meeting and Gael was aware of the keen advantage. He'd been thinking it over and had reached his decision. It would be better to go it alone if he could but with a power base no broader than peasant farmers, no more potent than students who had no future, he doubted he could retain an authority which for the moment derived from nothing more than a clause in a paper constitution. But with Gael he would have the South behind him and what he most feared, the power of the army. The embattled North might call general strikes but the army could deal with general strikes. Gael Milo was a prize to be captured and later, if she turned tiresome, he'd ditch her.

He showed no sign of the thought as he gave her the flowers. 'My absence from your husband's funeral was a mark of respect for his private wishes.'

'I know it,' Gael said.

'I thank you for that.'

He realized all this was distinctly formal but decided to stay with the formal manner. The fastidious considered it very inelegant but it could grease the wheels of a difficult interview, a shield between his real intentions and a woman he intended to use. Besides, he had a wellfounded rule: what the fastidious hated was mostly serviceable.

Gael too had a reason to welcome formality. This man was her husband's heir to power but he'd succeeded by an assassination. So far the boy, still held by the police, had insisted that he'd acted alone. Gael decided he'd been rather unlucky. If he'd only been a better shot he might have got away with it but he'd had to fire three which was two too many. Three shots had alerted a plain-clothes policeman and given him time to see where they came from. The boy had come tearing down the stairs and straight into the policeman's arms.

But so far Milo's stringent rules—no beatings, no starvings, no physical torture—had been respected since no one had dared to rescind them. The student had stuck to his story stubbornly: he'd been acting alone out of hatred of Milo. Gael considered this something less than probable but she knew that she couldn't prove a negative. But she also knew there were men besides students with more urgent motives to kill her husband.

One of them was now sitting with her.

'May I wish you well in your difficult duty?'

'It's not going to be an easy first year.'

'Political assassination is something which is often catching.' It was a statement of the utmost brutality and he answered at once as she'd known he would.

'I'm not afraid of assassination.'

'What are you afraid of?'

'The collapse of my country. That it will tear itself to pieces internally.'

It was the opening she had been waiting for. 'If I can help you in any way I will.'

He began to talk smoothly; he had chosen his words. She could help a great deal, indeed he was asking it. She had brought to her husband a very great dowry, the goodwill of the feudal South and its army. She still had that dowry intact and potent. It was true she was no longer active in politics but she sat in the People's House for the South, the mystique of her mother's name was still green. She could give again what she'd brought to Milo.

Kamich said this with the simple conviction of a man who was stating established facts and at the end he put it as more than suggestion: 'You'd be an asset to any man called on to rule.'

'Even to one whose views I hate?'

'Naturally there would be give and take.'

'You're suggesting a sort of diarchy?'

'I much prefer to call it alliance.'

'There'd be certain purely personal difficulties.'

He knew what she meant and didn't comment. The country would stand for split rule if it had to but hardly rule split between man and woman. The North would suspect some plot against it and the North earned the exports on which they lived. As for the South it wouldn't accept it. It would fly against all its ancestral instincts.

It would, that is, if the rulers concerned were simply a man and the other a woman. But if they also had a private relationship, one sanctified by a formal act, the South would consider that perfectly proper.

Kamich waited for Gael to go on but she didn't. At last he said: 'I can follow your thoughts.'

'You haven't yet made me a proposition.'

'I very gladly do so now.'

'You must realize I do not find it attractive.'

He considered invoking duty again, her duty to this unstable country, but he knew she was a realist too. Instead he said: 'All power has its compensations. Great ones.'

'And the personal aspect?' she asked.

'Purely formal.'

'I have your assurance of that?'

'Of course you have.' He said it without offending his conscience.

'I'll consider your proposition carefully.'

'You realize that if it's done at all it will have to be done with a certain dispatch.'

'I realize that.'

'The alliance publicly sealed and quickly.' Now surer, he had begun to press her.

'You put it,' she said, 'with your usual tact.'

'When may I know?'

'I will tell you tomorrow.'

She showed Kamich out and sat down unsmiling. It was better to act before the doubtings. She was inclined to think that he hadn't killed Milo, or not in the sense that he'd ordered the murder. But he might very well have known of the plan and if he'd done nothing then where was the difference?

166

Truth lay in the mouth of a single student.

Magda brought Russell's lunch and said after it:
'My mistress would like to see you at once.'
He had seen Gael only once since the shooting when
she'd pressed him very hard not to leave her. He hadn't
had any wish to stay, but if his presence gave her comfort
he wasn't the man to withdraw it abruptly even though
his firm was pressing him. He'd had two telegrams now
and had answered the second with a bland request to
extend his leave. If Gael thought of him as a surrogate
father that relationship was the more important, but this
almost peremptory summons surprised him.
He found her at Milo's modest desk, composed with a
sort of white hot calm. He had seen her before when her
mood was formidable; now she was something more. She
was desperate.
She led him to a car outside and Magda got in beside
the driver. Charles Russell asked her:
'Where are we going?'
'We're going to a police station.'
'Which?'
'The one which is holding Milo's murderer.'
'He hasn't talked yet?'
'That's why we're going.'
'What you're thinking of is risky,' he said.
'I know it's risky. Just the same we are going.'
'Milo made very strict rules.'
'He's dead.'
At the station a sergeant saluted smartly. 'Are you in
charge?'
'I am,' he said. 'And at your service.'

'I'd like to see an officer, please.' Normally she was a tactful woman.

The sergeant used an intercom and in a minute a Captain of Police appeared. Since he wasn't wearing a cap he clicked. 'Can I help you?' he inquired politely.

'You are holding a certain man here?'

'We are.'

'Has he spoken yet?'

'He has not spoken.'

'Kindly take me to his cell at once.'

The Captain hesitated, turning to Russell. He spoke no English but Gael translated. Charles Russell considered, then said to Gael: 'Please tell him I advise him to do so.' He liked neither Gael Milo's drawn face nor her manner. Besides, he had noticed her handbag fearfully. It was a large one and though he might be wrong he had the impression that it weighed more than usual. In her present mood she was not responsible but in the quiet of a cell he might hope to cool her.

The Captain led them to a cell in the basement, Gael Milo first, then Russell and Magda. The student was lying down on a bed. There was a policeman on a chair who stood up but at a word from the Captain he left the cell. Gael said to the Captain:

'Leave us, please.'

The Captain turned to Russell again, his manner a mixture of fright and petition. Gael Milo translated again for Russell.

'I cannot give you orders, you know, but I can offer you a long experience. If I were in your place I'd do as she says. I'd think it the lesser of two grave dangers and if anything happens I'll speak for you later.'

'I thank you, Colonel.' The Captain left them.

The boy had begun to climb off the bed but Magda promptly knocked him back on it. Gael opened her bigger than normal bag, producing not a gun but a rope. She gave it to Magda.

'Tie him securely.'

Magda did so.

The boy lay there, visibly sweating, terrified. He'd been interrogated for two full days but he'd held against mere interrogation. This was going to be something entirely different.

Gael Milo walked over and stood by the bed. 'You will tell me whom you were working for.'

Silence.

'You're not the type to stand much pain.'

The boy said: 'I did it alone.'

'On whose orders?'

Again there was silence: Gael opened her bag again. She took from it her mother's knife, wetting a finger and feeling the edge.

The boy's eyes had begun to glaze in terror.

Suddenly Gael leant forward smoothly. She nicked the boy's neck in a three-inch wound but she'd been careful to miss the jugular vein.

She knows her anatomy, Russell thought. Most Southerners did. Their fathers taught them.

She stood there waiting, as calm as a surgeon. If she was feeling a natural hatred she was showing no sign of emotion whatever. She was as impassive as a professional hangman.

She raised the knife again and the student screamed. There was a bang at the door but Magda had bolted it.

'Tell me,' Gael said.

He began to blubber.

She nicked him again, the other side. 'Next time it won't be your neck.' She gestured.

The boy managed to get his hands there. 'No.'

'I decide that and there isn't a remedy.' She balanced the knife again. 'Better to tell me.'

'Kamich,' he said through his sobs.

'I feared it.'

Gael looked at the knife but then put it away. 'That's hardly worth another notch.'

In the car going back to Milo's palace her mood had swung with a sudden violence which Russell's instinct was to mistrust profoundly. She was as gay as a bird in a summer tree.

'You seem as happy as a bride at a wedding.'

'I *am* getting married,' she said.

'I'm hurt.'

'You mean that I didn't tell you before? But I've only just decided this minute.'

'May I ask who's the fortunate man?'

'It's Kamich.'

'I simply don't believe what you say.'

'You think I am joking?'

'You *must* be joking.'

'I'm not joking in any way. I'm serious.'

'But that boy said——'

'I heard him.'

Charles Russell was out of his depth and showed it. 'You'd marry your husband's murderer?'

'Certainly.'

'It doesn't sound right to an Englishman.'

'Quite. But then, you see, I'm not an Englishman. I have different blood and quite different traditions. Also I'm not a man, I'm a woman.'

He tried again. 'But it doesn't make sense.'
'It makes excellent sense. It makes it much easier.'
'Makes what easier?'
'What I have to do.'

14

The wedding had been a civil one, for though religious weddings were not illegal they were unfashionable in ruling circles, regarded as an old-fashioned obeisance to superstition which was no longer relevant. At the glum town hall there'd been only two witnesses, the General and Charles Russell himself. The bride and bridegroom had driven back to the palace and Russell and the General had followed in an army car.

Russell had gone to his room to pack, happy that he could leave next day with excuses for not obeying its orders which any board in the land must surely accept. But the General had gone to talk to Gael Kamich. His instructions to do so had been sent to him earlier.

They'd been instructions but his reception was warm. Both he and Gael had a common blood, both had a similar background and ethos. What a Northerner would have thought outrageous was to both of them normal and sometimes praiseworthy.

'I must thank you for being a witness.'

'A privilege. Also a show of the army's support.'

'I'm afraid I've surprised you by marrying Kamich.'

'Not at all. You'll remember I once presumed to hint to you.'

She smiled. 'Are you telling the truth? Or all of it?'

'Since you press me I'm not telling all of it. No.'

'And the bit you are hiding?'

'Surprise at the speed of it.'

'You think that was unseemly?'

'No. Necessity has its own grim rules.'

'I noticed you said "necessity". A non-Southerner would have said simply "politics".'

'A non-Southerner would have been wrong,' he said.

'What are you trying to hint to me now?'

'I am not trying to hint, I will tell you straight. I told you once we had good Intelligence. It doesn't run to bugging police cells but it does run to knowing Gael Kamich's movements.'

'So you know I went down to see that prisoner?'

'Accompanied by a Colonel Russell and an ex-sergeant from the Regiment of Women. The Colonel I know by reputation and the ex-sergeant I have had carefully checked. Her record was a very tough one.'

'But you don't know what happened inside that cell?' He shook his head. 'But I might make a guess.'

'There is no need to guess. He gave me a name.'

'The name of the man who really murdered your husband?' He corrected himself. 'I mean your late husband?'

'I have only one husband. I very much loved him.'

As answer he put on his cap and rose. He gave her a tremendous salute. A British drill sergeant would have passed it approvingly and indeed he had learnt it from just that source. He said obliquely though she understood him: 'If there's one thing I admire above others it's a woman who will respect a custom.'

'I'm happy you understand me, General. And discharging a debt by another hand is poor satisfaction to people like us.'

'The old ways are sometimes the best—I concede it.'

'In this case?'

'I haven't a doubt at all.'

When he sat down they had both relaxed. The General accepted a malt Scotch whisky. It was his favourite drink and Gael was hospitable. Now they were calmly discussing their plan, the amendments which would now be necessary.

'You told me you wanted double harness. What happens if the mare runs alone?'

'I should support her,' he said, 'since needs I must. There isn't an alternative, or nothing which the South would accept.'

'And the terms of that support?'

'No terms. I told you I'm not ambitious politically. If I had been,' he added, a trifle grimly, 'you wouldn't now be alive to ask me.' He accepted another whisky gracefully. 'But there are certain things I must do at once and the timing is very important indeed. Too early and I may frustrate your intentions, too late and there's going to be serious rioting.'

'I cannot time it precisely.'

'I do not ask it.'

'Let us say between half-past eleven and midnight.'

The General rose and looked at his watch. 'That gives me adequate time to move, or at any rate to move armoured units. Naturally I shall do so discreetly. They will halt two miles outside the town and at half-past eleven will start to move in.'

Charles Russell had gone quietly to bed but he hadn't supposed he'd be able to sleep. He was lying in bed, hands behind his head, when Magda burst into the room abruptly. She was carrying her efficient Lüger.

'My mistress wants to see you again.'

'Whatever for?'

'To see fair play.'

174

'It's a fallacy Englishmen love fair play. We put the story about to our own advantage.'

'This isn't a moment for foolish talk.' She made a gesture with the efficient Lüger. She didn't precisely point it at Russell but it was clear she was prepared to do so. She was excited and she was also determined.

He got out of bed and put on a dressing-gown, following her along endless corridors. She stopped at a door and rapped on it firmly. Gael Milo opened: they both went in. Kamich was in the single bed, his expression a mixture of fear and astonishment. A man was covering him with another pistol but at a word from Gael he left the room. Magda had turned her Lüger on Kamich.

Charles Russell considered: weight of arms was against him. Magda had a pistol out and Gael Milo held her mother's knife. Besides, he didn't like the look of Gael, her face was set in a sort of ecstasy. The hair on the nape of his neck rose in protest but intervention would be very unwise. He said as mildly as he could make himself do so:

'You're not going to shoot him?'

'I'm not unless he's entirely chicken. I'm going to give him a chance to kill me. That's why you're here. You're a referee.'

'I beg to decline the honour.'

'You cannot.' She said something to Magda who shifted the pistol. Her eyes were shining with more than excitement. Like Gael she was standing in rapture, a second priestess at some unholy rite. Charles Russell was very scared indeed.

Gael Milo produced another knife, the twin of her mother's in weight and reach. She threw it on the bed and waited.

The man in the bed made no movement to take it.

'Barbarous,' he said. 'You're a savage.'

'Whom you married after killing my husband.'

'I deny it,' he said.

'You're a fool and a coward.'

'I'm not going to fight with a knife—a woman.'

'If you don't you're going to die by a bullet.' She said something to Magda again who fired twice. Both bullets thumped into the pillow solidly, one a foot to the left of Kamich's head, the other an equal foot to the right.

Instinctively Kamich had jumped off the bed but he'd made no movement to take the knife.

'Pick it up.'

'You're insane.'

The third bullet missed his head by an inch. He put out his hand, then he drew it back.

Gael Milo said to Magda: 'To kill.'

Kamich picked the knife up slowly.

Charles Russell wasn't aware of banality. In fact he had simply said: 'What next?'

Magda answered him. 'We shall keep to the rules.'

Gael had been talking to Kamich softly. He'd been standing in his dressing-gown.

'Take that dressing-gown off.'

He took it off.

She'd been standing in her dressing-gown too and she slipped from it herself to face him. She was beautiful, Charles Russell thought, but it wasn't her beauty which froze his brain. He couldn't have intervened if he'd dared, this was ancient and evil but deeply rooted. Somewhere under his civilized skin an instinct stirred in reluctant response.

Kamich had been standing immobile but now he was suddenly shaken by fury.... To be so close, to be tripped by this. 'You're an animal,' he said.

'I'm a widow.'

He went at her in a clumsy rush. Gael Milo's feet hadn't seemed to move but the thrust had missed by at least a foot.

'Please do better than that.'

He came again. This time she blocked his forearm neatly, then slipped inside and slashed his face. She cut it twice, once up, once across. There were two livid weals in the form of a cross.

Charles Russell had escaped from his trance; he was civilized again and English; he said sharply : 'Not to play with him, please.'

Perhaps she heard and perhaps she did not. Kamich was standing half-blinded, panting. Gael made a simple feint and closed. Kamich went down in a heap on the floor.

Charles Russell sat down on the bed; he was shaken.... A modern almost westernized country and its women would fight with knives like men, with another man, to avenge their husbands. Magda had begun to sing softly, a Lydian air sounding vaguely Turkish. Well, her country had once been a Turkish *banat*. He couldn't tell if she sang in grief or triumph.

He turned to Gael, bending over Kamich. She had withdrawn her mother's knife and was holding it. He had noticed that she fought left-handed but she was holding it with the other hand. With her left she picked up the second knife and with it began to cut at her mother's. She was chipping at the deerhorn handle, adding a sixth notch to the five.

Charles Russell heard his own voice faintly. It was calling on a God he'd abandoned. He sat down again and he looked at his watch. The time was exactly ten to midnight.

Outside there was the rumble of armour.

15

Charles Russell went quietly back to his room, now more certain than ever he wouldn't sleep. He made himself tea in the kitchenette and settled to wait for the dawn in a chair. He would have confessed he was severely shaken; he'd seen violence on much larger scales but there'd been something about the scene he'd just witnessed unmatched in the range of human passions. A referee, she had called him, had she? What she'd done had been a good deal more final than anything in professional football.

In the melee of conflicting emotions he realized that regret had come uppermost. It was possible to condone such acts, smothering them in the flannel of cliché, particularly something called natural justice, but such excuses were only effective if felt—deep in your private and secret viscera, bred in your bones as in Russell's they weren't. A man who didn't feel like that was contemptible if he played with words, but nor need he wallow in moral judgement, a failing as alien to Russell's mind as whitewashing what he thought was a crime. But regret was a perfectly valid emotion, regret for the act and regret for Gael Milo. Charles Russell had admired her greatly and once he had loved Gael's mother. Now he knew that he'd never see her again.

He wondered how when the sun came up she and that General would meet their crisis. He'd only met him at that dreadful wedding but he had recognized the type at once, the hard-headed and very efficient soldier. No doubt they couldn't hide Kamich's body as Gael Milo had told him they'd hidden Bojalian's. Had that death been another and final factor in driving Kamich to his attempt at power, the fear what Bojalian's masters might do if his death was left unexplained to insult them? Charles Russell shook his head; he would never know.

So they couldn't just hide a body with knife wounds but nor would there be a public inquest. This wasn't that sort of country at all. That General had struck him as good at his staff work; he suspected that Kamich was boxed already, the coffin slipped up by discreet back stairs. Thereafter there'd be a trustworthy doctor with a certificate of some form of seizure. Such incidents were by no means unknown, a man of a certain age, not an athlete, determined to prove that he was and failing. The people of this vigorous land might hide smiles but they wouldn't assume a lie. Then the General would go on the air at once, appealing for calm and very probably getting it since it was clear his troops now controlled the capital. But he'd appeal for rather more than calm, he'd ask for sympathy and might get that too, sympathy for a woman twice widowed. He would deny any private ambition whatever. Milo had held the country together and all he was doing was guaranteeing that till a dangerous situation cooled.

Would the two of them contrive success? Charles Russell rather thought they would. It was certainly important they should. Gael would continue her husband's policies and those had included a contract with Commonwealth. That contract had been to exploit iron ore: now it was that dynamite gold. Russell didn't yet know what his chairman had done, that a company calling itself Mid

Western now effectively controlled his own, but Gael had told him of an ambassador's visits and he knew a great Power now stood behind them.

That was going to be more useful than sympathy which in any case might not be forthcoming. There was a newspaper published north of London which would be instantly and severely critical. It would see this as a straight military takeover. The lights were going out again and all registered readers of liberal habit must react in an unqualified protest. When it heard that it was gold, not iron, something it would discover much later by reading livelier papers with better news services, it would see it as a bankers' ramp, particularly American bankers. Charles Russell smiled a tolerant smile. These thunderings were by now sad wind since nowadays very few readers heard them, but it was sad that in all Charles Russell's country he couldn't name a newspaper which would handle it as he thought it should be. This may be good for us—rejoice and be thankful. Happily none of this was important. Newspapers didn't make foreign policy and those who did had an evident interest in giving Gael Milo a run for her money.

Charles Russell allowed another smile. In most of his previous small adventures he'd been left with a handful of ends to tidy. In this one he need do nothing whatever. All he need do was return to London and give wise advice as he always did.

Still he couldn't sleep and he didn't try to. A woman might have relaxed his tension but that wasn't an amenity to be found in Gael Milo's unusual *ménage*.

Lord Tokenhouse looked round his boardroom table. He had prepared his statement with very great care though he knew it was going to be less what he said than the manner in which he put it over. So he offered no apology, no apology of any kind. Milo had extracted a promise, and though it might be arguable that their chairman should not have given it, the final sanction against a director's misjudgement was a General Meeting to vote him out. Short of that he had every intention of staying, and for reasons which would appear rather later such a meeting was very likely to fail.

Meanwhile Milo's death had discharged the promise—Milo's death and various other matters. The first was that this was gold, not iron. Commonwealth Mining was now big league, and let that be remembered, please, in any criticism of his previous actions. They were, after all, a business house, and business could not be run like a Sunday School. As for the fact of Mid Western's control, their chairman came close to welcoming that. Gold was very different from iron, different in kind as well as in value. It had international overtones and if it fell in wrong hands could do desperate damage. So was there not at least a case for welcoming a powerful ally, an ally with real muscle behind him? For the Board's information there were people who thought so. Their chairman was going to New York tomorrow, where of course he'd be meeting Mid Western's President, and that chairman wouldn't be flying alone. A British Minister was going too and a team of assorted civil servants, the hardboiled ones, not the wets from the Foreign Office. This was politics, top level policy, not a matter of digging up metal and selling it.

So Lord Tokenhouse looked round his board though he knew in advance how each man would feel. Macrae would see profits; he was paid to see profits; he would also wish to consult with Russell whose return was expected the

following evening. Weston, as ever, would go with the
meeting, waiting for a lead from the others. Only Shaw
had lost face and Shaw might niggle.

'This is very surprising news,' he said.

'Surprising but in my view happy.'

'I have very little knowledge of gold.'

'I don't think that of the least importance. A man with
your record and great experience can learn new techniques
in a matter of weeks.'

And in any case, Lord Tokenhouse thought, Mid
Western had other and first class men.

'In that case——' Shaw said.

Lord Tokenhouse rose.

Charles Russell's reflections were broken rudely by a
knock on his cautiously bolted door.

'Who's there?'

Magda's voice said: 'It's only me.'

He let her in and she stood silently watching him. He
could see that like himself she was strained, and she confirmed it by saying:

'Not able to sleep.'

'But I notice you're learning more English words.'

'I buying a little book.' She waved it. 'You not sleeping
too.'

'I am certainly not.' He considered the moment. 'Not
on duty?' he asked her. 'I mean, not working?'

Magda shook her head and waited.

'I would say you had earned a rest. How much rest?'

'Till tomorrow,' she said with care.

'It's enough.'

She began to peel neatly, quick and conclusively. When
she was naked she got into bed.

... They are certainly a forthright people.

Charles Russell took off his dressing-gown and sat down on the bed, not yet decided. No lack of zeal stayed immediate action but Magda was still holding her book.

'What book is that?'

'It is phrase book of English.'

Charles Russell was a little put out. He'd made love in some very curious circumstances, lying out in the hills with Gael Milo's mother, in a gondola after he'd ditched its owner, in the plush bedrooms of Johannesburg's rich. But he'd never yet made love by phrase book. He said in a voice of resignation:

'The postilion has been struck by lightning.'

'Pardon?'

'You don't ever say "Pardon" alone. But never. You say "Sorry" or if you want to be formal it's permissible to say "Beg your pardon".'

She didn't understand but laughed. She showed no sign of impatience, she was perfectly sure of him. She fluttered the phrase book's tattered pages, exposing an ample charm as she did so. It came open at one which was headed *Hotels*.

'This hotel is good.'

'I agree. But curious. For a hotel some very odd things happen.'

'What does "change" mean, please?'

'*Cambiare*,' he told her.

'Here they changing the sheets every day and night.'

'And why do they do that?'

She giggled.

He rose from the bed, took the phrase book from her. He threw it on the floor and kicked it. 'That's a bloody book.'

'That is very bad word.'
He had joined her in the double bed. 'I know nicer ones.'
He began to use them.